KM

20-12·2011

~~NOTION~~ 2/15

LCL 12/15

BPL
O4/16

1 4 NOV 2018

**Cumbria Library Services**

County Council

This book is due for return on or before the last date above.
It may be renewed by personal application, post or telephone,
if not in demand.

C.L. 18F

# Guarding Grace
# REBECCA YORK

First published in Great Britain 2011
by Mills & Boon, an imprint of Harlequin (UK) Limited,
Large Print edition 2011
Eton House, 18-24 Paradise Road,
Richmond, Surrey TW9 1SR

© Ruth Glick 2010

ISBN: 978 0 263 21791 9

Harlequin (UK) policy is to use papers that are natural, renewable and recyclable products and made from wood grown in sustainable forests. The logging and manufacturing process conform to the legal environmental regulations of the country of origin.

Printed and bound in Great Britain
by CPI Antony Rowe, Chippenham, Wiltshire

Award-winning, bestselling novelist Ruth Glick, who writes as **Rebecca York**, is the author of more than one hundred books, including her popular 43 Light Street series for Mills & Boon® Intrigue. Ruth says she has the best job in the world. Not only does she get paid for telling stories, she's also the author of twelve cookbooks. Ruth and her husband, Norman, travel frequently, researching locales for her novels and searching out new dishes for her cookbooks.

# *Prologue*

The assassin never left murder to chance.

Night was the best time for the mission he had taken on, which was lucky for the working stiffs who toiled at Bio Gens Labs.

Only one car was in the parking lot, a silver Mercedes occupying the choice reserved spot beside the employees' entrance.

With his headlights off, he slid in beside it and cut the engine of his rental car.

He had stowed his luggage in the trunk and started the evening with a nice prime-rib dinner at Ruth's Chris Steak House in downtown Bethesda, Maryland, only ten miles away.

Soon he would leave his calling card in this long low building and speed away. Some men would have been too nervous to eat before a big job. He found a full belly added to his feeling of satisfaction.

This was his fourth carefully calculated hit—and the most important. Massachusetts, California and New Jersey had just been rehearsals. With the widely separate locations, nobody had connected the dots. No one knew who had struck a federal judge, a U.S. congressman and a movie producer. Nobody knew who was next. Or why.

Gym bag in hand, he walked through the misty evening to the lab's delivery entrance. He had clocked the schedule of the security staff who patrolled the grounds of the industrial park. Nobody would be back along this route for twenty minutes.

The lab had a silent alarm, of course. But that didn't mean squat. By the time the Montgomery County Police Department responded, the place would be history.

After setting down his bag, he got out his stainless-steel lock picks. "The Navy SEALs' choice," according to the catalog from which he'd purchased the set.

He'd put in hundreds of hours of practice with these implements.

*One pin at a time. Apply force. Find the pin that is binding the post and push it up.*

Once inside, he set his gym bag on the receptionist's desk and removed the explosive device. It was a carefully constructed work of art. Too bad he was the only living person who would see it in such pristine form.

The exterior tubing was made of thick metal. The inside had a plastic liner, designed to hold the explosive mixture—a simple combination of ground aluminum and carbon tetrachloride that would reduce this room and the office beyond to a heap of debris.

He would have liked to use a military fuse. But he never bought his bomb-making materials from sources that could be traced. So he was using one designed for fireworks.

He lit the fuse and glided toward the executive suite at the end of the hall. In an elegantly furnished room fifty feet away, a small man wearing a wrinkled dress shirt bent over his computer keyboard. His dark hair was shot with gray now. His shoulders were slightly hunched. And he was unaware that he had only minutes to live.

Yet some sixth sense pulled the doctor's attention away from the computer screen.

"Who's there?"

Whirling in his chair, he turned to face the door—then froze when he saw the figure blocking the exit—bomb in hand.

"Who the hell are you? What are you doing here?" he demanded with the arrogance of a man who thinks he's the one in charge.

"I'm one of your children, Dr. Cortez. Don't you recognize me?"

A jolt of fear flashed in the doctor's eyes as he reached for the telephone.

The assassin's reflexes were excellent. He leaped across the room, kicking Cortez away from his desk, toppling his chair and spilling him onto the tile floor. The doctor lay stunned for a moment, then reached to clasp the back of his head. His palm came away covered with blood.

The intruder moved farther into the room, staying out of the man's reach, the bomb held up like a football ready for a touchdown pass.

Cortez's gaze flicked from his bloody hand to the intruder's face, to the bomb with its fuse burning steadily down toward the payload.

"Don't," he whimpered.

A fierce explosion cut off his plea. Ending two lives—and thirty years of diabolical scientific research.

# Chapter One

*Six months later*

Grace Cunningham picked up her briefcase and walked into the closet-size room that held the copy machine.

She hated hanging around after her stint in this office was finished. But, if anybody asked, she had a good reason to be here. The last time the great man who'd hired her to organize material for his autobiography had mislaid some of her notes, he'd cost her hours of work. This evening, she wanted her own copy of the research summary.

He'd left her at nine, as he always did, and

she had no illusions about why. He was using her as a cover to meet another woman. And they weren't working on his book. Unless he was planning a chapter on "sexual conquests."

But as a junior research assistant with a day job at the Smithsonian, Grace wasn't in a position to complain.

Everybody in her office kept telling her how lucky she was to score this assignment. She didn't bother filling them in on the level of stress.

She'd thought he was taking his honey farther down the hall. But when intimate laughter drifted through the wall from the adjoining office, Grace went rigid. She didn't want to hear what was going on in there, but she couldn't turn off the lurid pictures that suddenly flashed into her mind.

The client was a man of immense power in the capital of the free world. A guy who worked behind the scenes in ways the public couldn't even imagine. Although a few knew his name, they felt his influence. Only in his late fifties, he was starting to worry about his health.

Grace had seen the woman—a blonde much younger than her lover. Young enough to flatter his ego.

Her low, throaty voice drifted through the closed door. "I have an idea you'll want to try."

Grace's insides clenched. Her mother hadn't raised her to listen in on a scene like this.

She turned off the copy machine and then the light as a man wearing a business suit stopped in the corridor outside the next-door office and gave the closed door a smirking look.

Obviously he knew what was going on in there, too.

Feeling her face redden, she took a step back into the shadows, hoping he hadn't seen her and wouldn't think she was eavesdropping. Every muscle in her body tensed as she listened to the sound of rustling clothing and panting breath through the connecting door.

Each minute that ticked by felt like a century.

Finally she heard the moans of a man reaching orgasm.

Thankful that her unwanted stint as a voyeur was over—she went still when the cry of satisfaction changed to a loud gasping sound of pain.

The man she'd seen in the hall ran through the office where Grace was standing and charged through the connecting door into the room where the lovers were closeted. He was shouting something that sounded like, "Ridgeway is down! Repeat. Ridgeway is down!"

Obviously the guards had gone into panic mode. Seconds later, more footsteps came pounding down the hallway.

The door between the two offices was open, giving Grace an excellent view of what was going on inside. She pressed her fist against her mouth. A few moments ago she'd been embarrassed by the sounds of lovemaking. Now she was grappling with something far worse.

Armed bodyguards kicked open the hall door

and shoved their way into the office where the man lay unmoving on the beige carpet.

"Get a doctor," one of them shouted into the microphone at his collar. "He's unconscious. Get the defibrillator."

A man holstered his weapon and sprinted into the hall, reappearing moments later with a plastic case. Someone else started CPR.

Grace shrank into the shadows, her heart pounding as she stared at John Ridgeway, head of the Ridgeway Consortium, one of the most prestigious think tanks in DC. This morning he'd been advising the president. Now he was lying gray and unconscious in a back office of the consortium's downtown headquarters.

*Oh God.*

Her gaze bounced around the room, and she saw Ridgeway's sex partner crouched in the corner, pulling up the bodice of her black dress to cover her small breasts.

The woman's gaze met Grace's for a couple of frantic heartbeats, then flicked to the right before settling on the bodyguard bearing down on her. Grace knew her name. It was Karen Hilliard.

The man grabbed Karen by the elbow and pulled her roughly to her feet.

"What the hell did you do?" he demanded, thrusting his face into hers.

She raised her chin. "Nothing. I haven't done anything. Let me go."

The man's hold on her arm tightened. "You're kidding, right?"

More footsteps came rapidly down the hall, and an older man with thinning dark hair and unstylish horn-rimmed glasses entered the scene of chaos. Grace recognized him at once. Ian Wickers, Ridgeway's chief of staff.

"What's happened?"

"Looks like a heart attack."

"Will he pull through?"

"Don't know. The doc's on his way."

Wickers turned to the guard who held the woman in place. "Take her to the secure room in the basement."

"Yes, sir."

The man hustled Karen out. After they were gone, Wickers addressed the room at large, his voice clipped and commanding. "Archer, zip up his fly."

One of the bodyguards kneeling over the unconscious man unceremoniously maneuvered his limp penis back inside his underwear and zipped up his pants.

Wickers kept talking. "Mr. Ridgeway was alone when he had a heart attack. I'm not going to have a scandal cloud the reputation of the consortium."

"Yes, sir," came a chorus of agreement.

From her hiding place in the next room, Grace watched the unfolding drama, her heart thumping. When her knees threatened to give way, she leaned back against the wall, grappling with her own disbelief.

It had all happened so fast. Too fast. She should have done something. But what?

Her brain threatened to shut down. But she forced herself to take deep breaths and stay cool.

One salient fact leaped out at her, grabbed her by the throat and wouldn't let go.

A cover-up.

She was a witness to a cover-up of major proportions. They'd hauled Karen Hilliard off to the basement and made it look as if John Ridgeway was alone and working late. What was going to happen to Karen Hilliard now? And what would these ruthless men do if they discovered another woman had seen everything? Heard everything. Would they let her live to tell about it?

Feeling as if she was standing on quicksand, she pressed her hand against the hard surface of the copy machine. If only she'd left the building when her research job was over, she'd be home by now.

The medics brought a stretcher and loaded the unconscious man onto it.

"Will he make it?" Wickers asked.

"He's already dead. Like Michael Jackson," the doctor answered.

After all the frantic activity, the room and

the hallway were finally empty. This might be her only chance to get away.

The security man who had seen her earlier had forgotten about her in the confusion. But when he started thinking clearly, he would remember there'd been a witness.

She wanted to run. But she forced herself not to panic. Two years ago she'd turned her life upside down and come to Washington on her own. If she could do that, she could get through this.

At least she'd caught one lucky break. She'd gone shopping with a coworker on her lunch hour at a couple of the boutiques on Seventh Street. Fumbling in her briefcase, she pulled out a black jockey's cap and jammed it onto her head, pushing her sable-colored locks out of sight.

She thought about hiding her blue eyes with sunglasses. But that would look strange at night.

Keeping her head down so the security cameras wouldn't pick up her face, she stepped out of the copy-machine room.

But she couldn't stop the death scene from playing out in her mind. She'd known Ridgeway had heart problems. And hidden them from the public. He was arrogant. And secretive. And he'd thought he could operate outside the laws of God and man.

She started to turn away. Then from under the sofa, she caught the glint of something that sparkled. As she stared at it, she remembered the split second when Karen had looked at her—then to her right. Toward the couch.

Every self-protective instinct screamed at Grace to get out of the building before it was too late. But instead of running in the other direction, she took a quick step toward the couch, then another. Reaching underneath, she felt something that wasn't part of the office equipment. It was Karen's beaded evening bag.

Had it gotten kicked there during the emergency? Or had Karen deliberately hidden it? Why? As proof of what had happened?

Or maybe she'd understood Grace's dilemma—and handed her a kind of insurance policy.

With shaking fingers, she shoved the evening bag into her briefcase. Conscious that she had to get out before they locked down the consortium complex, she stood and walked into the hall, striding to the exit as if she'd only been working late.

"See you next week?" the security guard asked, and she knew he wasn't in the loop.

"Yes," she managed to say in a cheerful voice as she turned in her badge, signed out and walked toward the gate that opened onto Pennsylvania Avenue, praying it was still open.

BRADY LOCKWOOD bent his muscular six-foot frame so that he could stare into the unpromising depths of the refrigerator, eyeing a red-and-white carton of kung pao chicken and half a Philly cheese steak.

How old were they, exactly? Probably old

enough to send his digestive system into spasms.

He tossed the takeout containers into the trash, then grabbed a bottle of ginger beer and took a swig, wincing as the sharp bite of the potent soft drink hit his mouth.

For the past three years he'd lived in Washington, DC, in La Fontana, one of the grand old apartment buildings that lined upper Connecticut Avenue.

Better get back to work, he told himself, heading for the office down the hall. He'd taken a new case this afternoon. Typical P.I. deadbeat-dad stuff. Not like the interesting assignments he'd gotten from the Light Street Detective Agency.

But that was then. This was now.

He'd just started thumbing through the files, when the phone rang. Although the ID didn't give the caller's name, the number told him it was the Ridgeway residence.

He braced to hear his brother asking for help with his latest mess.

Instead, John's wife expelled the breath she must have been holding. "Brady, thank God."

"Lydia, what's wrong?" he asked, picturing her delicate aristocratic features stiff with tension but not a strand of her dyed auburn hair out of place.

"I can't talk over the phone," she said, her control almost slipping. "Just come over here. I…need you."

*I need you.*

In the twenty-five years they'd known each other, she had never uttered those words. In public she could look friendly. But she'd never asked for his help. What was going on over there?

"I'm on my way."

Hurriedly, Brady changed from sweats into dark slacks and a button-down shirt. As an afterthought, he shrugged into a tweed jacket and paused to swipe a comb through his unruly dark hair.

On the ride up rain-washed Connecticut

Avenue, he felt the hairs on the back of his neck prickle. He reached for his cell phone, then drew his hand back. He couldn't call Lydia to ask what was wrong, not when she'd sounded so secretive. Was she going behind John's back? What?

As he wove in and out of traffic, his mind drifted to the strange workings of fate. And of genetics.

Brady might be the smarter brother, but it was John who had the ear of the U.S. President.

Brady's goals had been more modest. He'd seen what the quest for power did to a man, how it changed his values and warped his perspective. All he'd wanted was a fulfilling job, a comfortable life—and a wife and two kids.

His hands clenched on the wheel. Unfortunately, that had been too much to ask.

As he turned into the driveway of the Ridgeway estate, the man in the guardhouse gave him a grim-faced look. Before Brady could blink, a bank of bright lights switched on, momentarily blinding him.

"Get out of the car," a voice boomed. "Keep your hands in the air where we can see them."

# Chapter Two

Shadows moved behind the lights. Men. With guns—judging by the glint of metal.

"Out of the car," the voice boomed again. "On the double if you don't want to get your ass shot."

Brady stepped into the rain, blinking as the spotlights stabbed into his vision.

From behind the wall of light, he heard a familiar voice, Bill Giordano, the man who headed his brother's home security detail.

"It's okay, Taylor. He's Ridgeway's brother."

Brady was allowed to get back into the car, along with the security man, and they proceeded up a curving drive toward the fifty-room mansion his brother had bought ten years ago.

"What are you doing here?" Giordano said, speaking in the quiet tone that Brady knew meant watch out how you answer.

"Lydia called me. She said she needed me. What's going on?"

"There's no easy way to say this. Your brother is dead."

Brady managed to drag in enough air to say, "How?"

"Heart attack—we think," Giordano answered. "He was catching up on some work at the office before he and Lydia went to a reception."

"Doesn't the consortium have a doctor on staff?"

"And defibrillators. All the goddamn latest equipment. If they could have saved him, you know damn well they would have."

Brady nodded, trying to pull himself together.

Lydia was waiting for him in the upstairs family lounge. Her eyes were red-rimmed as she walked toward him, setting a glass on an end table as she crossed the room.

As if to mock the occasion, she was dressed for an evening reception in a long emerald gown that was the perfect color for her hair and skin.

When she embraced him, the scent of the liquor on her breath grabbed him as tightly as her arms, and a seductive thought wove itself into his mind. He could have a shot of bourbon. Just one. To get himself through the trauma of John's death.

*Stop it.*

One drink, and he was on a one-way trip to hell. No bourbon. No exceptions.

THE CAB PULLED up in front of Grace's apartment just off Dupont Circle. She already had a ten-dollar bill in her hand, which she handed to the cabdriver.

"Keep the change," she called as she hurried

through the drizzle to the front door of the converted brownstone. Once it had been a single residence. Now each floor had two apartments.

Her low-heeled shoes clattered on the un-carpeted wooden steps as she climbed to her second-floor unit, unlocked her front door and stepped into the small living room.

When she'd locked the door behind her, she stopped short, her stomach clenching as she looked around the shadowy room. She'd been strapped for cash when she came to DC, and she'd lovingly put together this refuge with more imagination than money. Her sofa and coffee table were from a secondhand shop in Adams Morgan. She'd found the worn Oriental rug and the wicker baskets at garage sales. And she'd rescued the Queen Anne end tables from the alley two steps ahead of the trash truck.

She'd thought she was making a home for herself. Now she knew she'd been kidding herself.

John Ridgeway's death had changed everything. Quickly she checked to make sure nobody was lurking inside the apartment.

BRADY EYED the security man hovering discreetly at the edges of the room. "Where can we talk privately?" he asked Lydia.

His sister-in-law turned, the taffeta skirt of her evening gown swishing as she led him down the hall to a bedroom that looked as if it could have graced a Louisiana plantation house.

She sank onto an antique curved-back sofa. Brady took a parlor chair opposite her. Her complexion was pale, but her eyes were fierce.

"Let's cut to the chase. I know John was seeing other women. He'd done it through most of our marriage. That's why he stayed late at work tonight."

He answered with a tight nod. John loved to brag about his conquests. Man-to-man. Never to his wife. And then there was the illegitimate son he'd asked Brady to locate—not that John had actually gotten in touch with the boy as far as Brady knew.

He pulled out the small notebook he always carried and started making terse, cryptic notes.

"We had a reception tonight. At the Cosmos Club. He said he wanted to get in a couple of hours of work first—on his autobiography. With that research assistant from the Smithsonian. Grace Cunningham. He's been seeing her for a couple of months."

Brady cleared his throat. "And his security men knew what he was really doing?"

"I assume so."

"When did he usually meet with Grace Cunningham?"

"From six to eight on Tuesdays. She should have been gone when he died. But his staff could be lying about that."

"Did he write her address or phone number in his book?"

Lydia stepped into the walk-in closet and came out carrying a manila folder.

When Brady opened it, he saw a picture of a young, appealing woman with dark, chin-length hair and blue eyes. She was pretty, but she certainly didn't look like a seductress. Maybe that was part of her charm for John. Behind the picture were several pages of personal background.

"Can I take this?"

"Yes."

"What about his address book?"

Lydia hesitated.

"Would you rather have John's brother check his contacts—or the DC police?"

Lydia left the room and returned with a small blue book, which she handed to him.

When a knock sounded at the door, he thrust the folder into the waistband of his slacks in back, where it was hidden by his sports jacket, and the address book into his pants pocket.

"Come in."

"Sorry to disturb you, ma'am," Giordano said. "We'll be making an announcement soon about your husband's death. You might want to change into a dark suit before the press shows up here."

Lydia looked down at her evening gown as if realizing that she was dressed for a formal reception.

Standing quickly, she took a moment to compose herself. When she spoke, her voice was well modulated. "Yes. I'll be right with you."

The door closed again, and she raised her eyes to Brady. "I want to know if one of his enemies killed him. I mean—did somebody send in a woman to cut off the blood flow to his carotid artery or something? You have to find out what happened."

"If I can, I will," he promised. He was really speaking to himself, not Lydia. He'd gotten used to cleaning up John Ridgeway's messes. Maybe he was too comfortable with that role.

What he did now depended on what he discovered—starting with Grace Cunningham.

GRACE WANTED to scream at Karen Hilliard. Instead she pulled off her business suit and pulled on jeans, running shoes and a dark T-shirt. Leaving her good clothes in a pile on the bedroom floor, she made for the kitchen. Because she didn't want to announce that she was home, she worked with only the illumination from a streetlight outside the window as she pulled the sugar canister out of the cabinet, then started digging in the white grains like a dog looking for a buried bone.

As her fingers closed around the legal-size envelope, she breathed out a small sigh. She was going to need the cash. No credit cards. Not in the name of Grace Cunningham.

Or Ginnie Cutler.

She'd buried Ginnie two years ago. Everybody she'd known from before she'd made her big decision thought she had died in a boating accident. Even her parents, and it still made her heart squeeze when she thought about how her death must have devastated them.

They didn't even have the solace of a grave site—after all the years of raising their daughter, of loving their daughter.

Scenes from her life flashed through her mind as she dashed down the hall to the bedroom.

She remembered the pink-and-white little girl's bedroom that had made her happy. Her eighth birthday party when she'd proudly taken eight friends out to lunch. The smile on Mom's face when her daughter had graduated from high school.

Her parents hadn't had a lot of money, but they'd showered their daughter with love and given her the confidence to take the road she traveled now.

She'd come to Washington with a carefully constructed new identity and a lot of optimism. Like those first-term congressmen who thought they were going to make a difference. You could check her driver's license, her Social Security number and her college transcript—from Barnard instead of Brown, where she'd really gotten her history degree. All the documents would testify to whom she was supposed to be. The background had stood up to even Ridgeway Consortium scrutiny. Not anymore. They'd go digging and find out that Grace Cunningham had never really existed.

But before that—they'd check the visitors' book and see when she'd left this evening.

When she'd escaped through the Pennsylvania Avenue exit, she'd barely been thinking about her next move. Now she knew she was going to have to disappear—again. And come back as someone else. If she had the cash to do it again.

Not that she'd committed a crime. She'd just been in the wrong place at the wrong time.

In the bedroom she switched on the television, turning the volume low, and caught the news on CNN.

They were reporting John Ridgeway's death. But nothing had changed about the story.

So much for honesty in the halls of power.

As she stared at the television set, she wanted to curl up in a ball on the bed and close her eyes. She wanted to wake up and find out the past hour was all a horrible dream. But it was real. Just like the nightmare of two years ago.

Only now a powerful man was dead, and she was a witness. And if she didn't want to end up like Karen, a secret detainee, she'd better get the hell out of here.

She was throwing clothing into a duffel bag when she heard the wooden stairs creak. Her hand on a pair of jeans, she went rigid, listening intently.

It could be one of the neighbors. Maybe nosy Mrs. Sullivan who was always peeking out her front door to see if Grace was bringing anybody home.

The next sound she heard was something metal sliding into the lock of her apartment door.

No knock. Nobody calling out, "Police. Open up."

For a second, she was too stunned to move. Then she shoved the money into her purse, along with Karen Hilliard's evening bag.

Without a second thought, she abandoned the

duffel bag in the middle of the bed, thrust open the window and climbed out onto the ledge.

She hated to take extra time. But an open window was a dead giveaway, so she turned to ease down the sash behind her.

Thank God she was in good shape from all those laps at the pool—and the fencing lessons she'd been taking.

After slinging her purse strap over her shoulder, she lowered herself by her hands and let go, landing with a thunk on the roof of the next building. As soon as she hit the flat surface, she sprinted toward the edge, skirting puddles of standing water.

Behind her, through the old glass, she heard footsteps running through her apartment—then men's voices.

"Where the hell is she?"

"Maybe she didn't go home."

"Where else would she go?"

Without looking over her shoulder, she kept moving across the gravel, then over the side of the building.

"She's on the roof."

"Don't let her get away."

Lord, who were these men? The DC cops? Or more likely John Ridgeway's private security force.

Either way, she was pretty sure that getting caught could be a fatal error.

Fear swelled inside her chest, making it hard to breathe. But she didn't break her stride until she came to the edge of the building. As she lowered herself over the side, she saw a man coming out the window.

Two of them had barged through the front door without announcing their presence. Was the other one going around back to cut her off at the pass.

She dropped to the roof of a garage, then to the alley.

"Stop her!"

Praying she could make it, she hurtled down the alley, her running shoes splashing through puddles of dirty water. Before she reached the car, a hand whipped out from the shadows and grabbed her shoulder.

Grace screamed, the sound coming to her above the roaring in her ears.

She'd almost made it—and now...

A man barked out a gruff order. "Hold it right there, sweetheart."

It wasn't necessary to fake terror. She was literally shaking in her shoes. "Please don't hurt me," she whimpered.

"I won't. If you come quietly."

*Oh sure.*

When he turned her toward him, she went still, pretending to comply, letting him think he had control of a woman too terrified to resist. But as she came around, she lashed out, whacking her elbow into his armpit the way they'd told her to do in self-defense class.

He was totally unprepared for the attack. Grunting, he dropped his hold on her shoulder.

Free of his control, she struck out with her

foot, catching him in the balls. He screamed as he doubled over.

But he wasn't the only one she had to worry about. Another man dropped over the side of the roof, charging toward her.

If she ran, she had no chance. So she played deer in the headlights, standing still and breathing hard, forcing herself to wait until he was almost on her. Then she moved, using her body weight to shove the first guy into the second.

They both went down.

A curse rang out behind her as she turned and sprinted away, knowing this was her last chance.

Her lower lip wedged between her teeth, she kept moving, braced for the pain of a bullet slamming into her back.

Instead, just as she turned the corner, another man stepped into her path, trapping her.

"Come on," he said.

As he took in her wide-eyed look, he snapped, "I'm not one of *them*."

"Then who?"

"The cavalry. Come on."

"Where?"

"Away. Let me help you, before they catch up with you."

With a gun in his hand, he gestured toward a car pulled up at the curb. The guy looked tough and capable but subtly different from the men who'd broken into her apartment. Making a split-second decision, she climbed into the car.

Her heart was pounding so hard that she thought it might break through the wall of her chest.

"Who are you?" she asked.

"It looks like I'm your bodyguard."

"I can take care of myself."

"You put up a good fight, but they would have gotten you in the end."

She sighed, eyeing him. "What's your name?"

"Brady Lockwood."

Oh Lord. She should have recognized him! But the photos she'd seen of him had been old. He hardly looked like the same guy.

"You're John Ridgeway's brother."

# Chapter Three

Brady drove toward Georgetown with no particular destination in mind. The one thing he knew was that going home wasn't an option at the moment. Despite claiming to be her bodyguard, he still didn't know if he was going to end up taking Grace Cunningham to the cops. And he sure as hell didn't trust her enough to let her into his apartment.

As she sat next to him, she radiated tension. Yeah, well, she should. She'd been involved in something pretty nasty this evening.

He saw her hands trembling. She was on

the edge, and maybe he could use that to his advantage.

Turning off Wisconsin Avenue, he pulled onto a side street and under a streetlight that gave him enough illumination to see her.

When the car came to a stop, she glanced around in alarm. "Where are we?"

"On the run. But you look like you could use a friend."

"I'm fine," she protested.

"Of course not. You've been through a rough couple of hours."

He cut the engine, then reached across the console and gathered her close, stroking his hands over her back and shoulders, then into her hair, feeling her tremble.

"Everything's going to be okay," he whispered.

She stayed rigid for a moment, then relaxed against him. As he kept stroking her, murmuring low, reassuring words, he was having trouble fitting her into the murder scenario he'd constructed on the way to her apartment. The picture he'd seen made her look like the soul of innocence. The woman clinging to him gave the same impression. Yet he'd also seen her dispatch a couple of tough guys in the alley. Let's not forget about that.

"I'm scared."

"Yeah. I understand."

He'd taken her in his arms for purely mercenary reasons, yet he couldn't keep himself from reacting to the softness of her skin, her light flower scent, the clean feel of her hair.

*Careful, Brady, he warned himself. This is no time to be taken in by a woman who could work her way into a weekly liaison with the head of the Ridgeway Consortium.*

Yet she didn't seem like one of John's honeys. He went for women who were flashier, blonder. Women who knew that John Ridgeway might be able to help them along in the world.

She was more like Brady's own type. A lot more. Or was it that he had stayed away from any romantic relationships for too long? And the first young, pretty woman who came

along was tugging at his emotions in unexpected ways.

He should distance himself from her, but he
stayed where he was, captured not only by the
physical attributes of the woman but also by a
sense of connection.

Her voice woke him up to reality.

"It wasn't a coincidence that you showed up
in the alley in back of my apartment."

"Yeah."

"How did you find me?" she asked.

"I stopped by my brother's house. He had
your address and your photo in a personnel
file."

"Okay."

He reminded himself that he should be the
one getting information, and he didn't want to
be staring over Grace Cunningham's shoulder
when he questioned her. He wanted to be looking into her eyes. Would they shift to the side
or stay steady?

Easing away, he asked, "Are you feeling
better?"

"Some."

"Who was after you?"

Her gaze turned inward as she considered the question. "I'm not sure. Could be security guards from the Ridgeway Consortium," she said in a flat voice.

"The news said my brother was alone when he died."

She moistened her lips. "That's a lie."

"Oh yeah? How do you know? Were you with him?"

"No."

"But you were having an affair with him," Brady said because he wasn't going to get sucked into feeling sorry for this woman. Or feeling anything. He'd said he was her bodyguard. But that was for his convenience, not hers.

Her eyes shot up to him and her voice turned hard as she said, "I was *not* having an affair with him. He didn't appeal to me that way."

"You just said you were with him when he died."

She gave him a glacial look. "That's not what I said at all. I said he wasn't alone. I wasn't with him. There's a difference."

He kept the questions coming. "You were supposed to be working on a research project with him, but you were really having a liaison."

"No," she said again. "He was using me for something else."

CHARLES HANCOCK WAS a man used to making life and death decisions—and collecting the huge fees his clients were willing to pay.

Tonight he sat on the leather sofa in the den of his McLean mansion. The floor-to-ceiling drapes were open, and he could look out over his property.

The television played softly across the room. One of those programs he liked on Animal Planet where a macho guy ran around jumping into alligator pools or sticking his hand into scorpion holes. Charles was always hoping one of the fools would get chomped to death. Or stung by a stingray, like that Australian guy.

The show was good background for cleaning his Glock model 17L, a sweet little handgun if he'd ever seen one.

He glanced at the clock. It was ten and time for Anderson Cooper. The boy came across as steady and reliable. Charles had made that a rule of his own life.

He had no illusions of his own power. Or his own tragedies. After his wife and son had died in a terrorist attack in Egypt, he'd vowed to devote himself to the greater good of humanity. As he saw it. His goal was a stable society—with power in the hands of the people who knew how to wield it.

He stayed in the background, quietly giving substantial amounts of money to causes he thought would make a difference. Like his college scholarship fund for disadvantaged kids. A lot of people had written them off, but he understood that the better chances those kids had in life, the more likely they were to stay out of trouble.

Charles switched channels then sat up straighter when he saw the concerned expression on Cooper's lean face.

"White House advisor John Ridgeway suffered a fatal heart attack this evening while catching up on some work in his office." The anchor's words hit him like rocks slamming against a cement wall.

Carefully Charles set the handgun on the table in front of him.

Ridgeway was dead. Supposedly he'd died alone in his office.

Charles's mind flashed back to November six months ago, when an intruder had blown himself up—along with Dr. Richard Cortez—at the Bio Gens Laboratories in Bethesda, Maryland.

Cortez had been a close friend and colleague. When he'd heard the news, Charles went back and looked at the deaths of some of his clients.

Pat Richmond in Massachusetts. Joe Barlow in California. Ted Pierson in New Jersey.

Richmond had died in a hit-and-run accident. Barlow had been at home when a burglar broke into his Beverly Hills mansion. Pierson had drowned in a boating accident.

He'd wanted to dismiss those deaths—and half a dozen others—as unrelated. That was before the pipe bomb at Bio Gens Labs. Two people had died. Cortez and someone else— presumably the bomber.

Charles had obtained a sample of the DNA from what was left of the bodies. And what he discovered had brought cold sweat to his skin.

The police had never solved that mystery. Now what about Ridgeway? Were the authorities going to get a crack at the case—or was a grand cover-up in motion?

"MAYBE YOU'D BETTER explain what you mean about his using you for something else," Brady said.

He watched Grace drag in a breath and let it out.

"I was in the office complex, but your brother was with another woman when he died. They went into another office together. They made love. Then he gasped, and I assume he had a heart attack. There must have been security guards right around the corner. As soon as it happened, a couple of them rushed in—followed by Ian Wickers who runs security at the Ridgeway Consortium."

"I know who Wickers is!" He glared at her. "You expect me to believe someone else was with my brother?"

"Earlier, I was working with him on notes for his autobiography. We had a standing appointment every Tuesday night."

Just what Lydia had told him.

"Did you know he was working on an autobiography?" Grace Cunningham asked.

"He hadn't shared that with me."

"Probably he didn't want to tell you anything until he had a publisher lined up."

That sounded pretty cynical. Yet the observation fit. John wouldn't want to make a big announcement until he'd signed a multi-million-dollar book contract.

She continued with her version of the evening's events. "After our sessions together, he always left me and went to meet someone else."

He kept his gaze fixed on her. "That's an interesting story. Why should I believe it?"

CHARLES HANCOCK TYPED in his password— Paladin. It was from an old TV show, where a guy in a black hat rode around the old west righting wrongs.

He'd loved the show when he was a kid. So he'd appropriated the title. Paladin wasn't the Lone Ranger. He didn't always play by the rules. But he got things done.

The way Cortez had.

The doctor's death had been a personal tragedy. But Charles would find the right man to take over the research. Someone with vision.

Someone who understood the importance of maintaining stability in the government of the United States—and ultimately the world.

All the Bio Gens protocols were in the computer. Waiting for the right moment to start the project up again.

But right now he was into damage control.

His source at the consortium had confirmed his suspicion that Ridgeway hadn't been alone when he'd suffered his fatal heart attack. It seemed that he'd been playing Russian roulette with his health. He'd been with a woman, but Ian Wickers was keeping that information inside the building.

Good. That suited Charles's purposes perfectly. The fewer people who knew what had really happened, the better.

He had the woman's name. Karen Hilliard. He drummed his fingers lightly on the computer keyboard. He hated giving in to conspiracy theory. However, in this case he knew it was justified. When you put Ridgeway's death together with the murders across the country and then the explosion at Dr. Cortez's lab you came up with an unfortunate pattern.

The man who had blown himself up—along with Cortez—had been a rare bird. He'd called himself Billy Carmichael. But that was the name he'd taken after he'd disappeared into thin air.

Charles knew his real identity from the DNA sample he'd obtained. Billy Carmichael was one of the babies who had been conceived in a petri dish at Bio Gens Labs—then sold to childless couples desperate for children. Couples who bore all the expenses of raising one of Cortez's little darlings yet didn't know what a remarkable youngster they sheltered.

He switched to another database—the children. He didn't usually go into it unless he had a request from one of his clients.

Now he plugged in Karen Hilliard's name. He didn't find her, but he had a pretty good idea who she was. Three years ago, one of the children—now grown—had gone missing. A young woman named Kate Winthrop.

Charles's eyes narrowed as he stared at the computer screen. He had no conclusive proof, but he'd be willing to bet that Kate Winthrop and Karen Hilliard were one and the same.

She'd been one of Cortez's more bizarre experiments. He'd brought her into the world just to prove he could do it. Really, she'd been of no real use to anyone.

And now Charles cursed himself for not getting rid of her when he'd had the chance.

Switching to e-mail, he sent a message to his Ridgeway Consortium contact. First he wanted a physical description of Karen Hilliard. And her DNA—if he could get it.

Had she been working with the man who had blown himself up—along with Dr. Cortez? Or was she on a private mission?

Either way, he needed answers. And if he got the wrong one, he would have to take drastic action.

BRADY WATCHED GRACE Cunningham glare at him.

"I'm not telling you a 'story,'" she said, punching out the words. "And you should believe me because I haven't jumped out of the car and started running."

"How about, you know, I'd catch you and bring you back."

"Maybe. Maybe not." She kept her gaze steady. "Tonight, your brother was in the office next door when he had a heart attack. After he died, Wickers told one of the agents to take the woman to the basement. While they were busy with her and with your brother, I managed to get out of the building."

"You'll pardon me if I'm having a little trouble connecting with this fantasy."

She shifted in her seat. She might be spinning him a story, but she was scared of something—and not necessarily of him.

Then there was the logic of the situation. If she'd really been in the same room with John when he'd died, could she have gotten away?

He studied her face. She looked familiar, but he couldn't place her. Had he seen her at one of the parties that John insisted on dragging him to? The parties where he watched people drinking cocktails and highballs.

She surprised him by saying, "Your brother spoke very highly of you."

He snorted. "My job was taking care of business he didn't want made public."

"Then maybe you can do one last thing for him."

"Which is?"

"Find out what really happened and expose the cover-up."

He kept his gaze on her, hoping his posture gave nothing away. On the way to Grace's apartment, he'd called Wickers, and the guy had blown him off. Maybe Grace Cunningham really was what he'd been praying for—to use a conventional phrase because he hadn't prayed in years. If she was willing to tell the truth. But he wasn't going to act too eager.

He lifted one shoulder. "Maybe it's better to leave it the way it is."

"You want Wickers and his pals to control the situation? When I got home—armed men were only a few minutes behind me. Then you came and rescued me." She sighed. "Or maybe I'm kidding myself. Maybe you've already pushed a secret buzzer on your cell phone, and they're coming for me now."

"Maybe," he answered and watched her shoulders tighten.

"One woman's already disappeared. The woman who was with your brother. Either she's still in the basement of the Ridgeway Consortium, or they've taken her somewhere else. Or she's already dead."

"Dead! I've only got your word that she exists."

She reached into the large purse that sat on her lap and pulled out an evening bag. "While the guards were busy, I took a big chance and grabbed this."

When she laid it on the console next to him,

he turned on the overhead light, then opened the bag. Inside was a wallet with a driver's license belonging to someone named Karen Hilliard. There were also a couple of credit cards, a library card and an auto-club card. He held up the driver's license. She was an attractive woman with large dark eyes, short cropped blond hair and a challenging look on her face. More John's type. Just as with Grace Cunningham, he felt as if he knew her—only in this case, the conviction was even stronger.

"Who is she?"

"I don't know much about her."

"This could belong to anyone," he said.

"Sure. I made the whole thing up—to get myself off the hook." She dragged in a breath. "There's got to be a record of her entering the building. Oh, wait—they would have wiped it out."

"Maybe we should have a talk with her."

"If you can get into the Ridgeway Consortium basement—or wherever they're holding her now. I could tell Wickers I know about her."

"That might shorten your life."

"You think your brother's chief of staff is desperate enough to kill?"

"If he thinks it's necessary."

Brady knew John had hired Wickers for his expertise, and his ruthlessness. Him and that other guy, Phil Yarborough, who had a background working for a mercenary company that had gotten in trouble in Iraq. Neither man was going to give up anything he thought he could keep private.

He made a split-second decision. "Come back to my apartment and we'll talk about it." He hoped he wouldn't be sorry.

## Chapter Four

Karen Hilliard looked around her bleak surroundings. She was huddled on a narrow bed in a storage room, but it might as well be a cell.

A guy named Phil Yarborough had already questioned her, and she'd stuck to her story about meeting John Ridgeway at a party and letting him seduce her. Yarborough hadn't believed her. She hadn't expected that he would. And she was braced for the interrogation to get rougher.

When the door opened, she willed herself to steadiness. Yarborough strode back into the basement room and slammed the door behind him. Crossing to her, he grabbed her by the shoulder, pulling her to her feet.

"What the hell is going on?" he bellowed.

Determined not to let him scare her, she raised her chin. "I can't answer that question until you tell me what you want to know—specifically."

He took a breath as he struggled for calm. "We ran your fingerprints."

"And?"

"They come up as a match for John Ridgeway." When she didn't deny it, he gave her a shake. "How did you manage it?"

"New technology."

"Which is?"

She shrugged. "I'm not all that technical. I just follow directions."

"So you're admitting that somebody sent you here—to kill John Ridgeway."

*Okay, time for plan B.*

"I'm admitting that somebody wanted me to contact Ridgeway."

"Who?"

"I don't know, exactly. My guess is that they have ties to the Middle East."

"What makes you think so?"

"They look Arabic."

"And why are you working with them?"

"Because I need money."

"You're lying."

"What makes you think so?" she asked, echoing his phrasing.

"You're too dedicated. You have your own agenda. What do you have to gain by defending an Arab terrorist group?"

"They said they'd kill me if I talked."

"Then you're caught between a rock and a hard place because I'm going to kill you unless you come clean with me."

"I can't tell you anything if I'm dead, can I?"

He led her to the chair in the room and pushed her down, then pulled out a pair of handcuffs. As he secured her wrists to the wooden arms, a tremor went through her.

Roughly, he turned her hand over and looked at the tips of her fingers, then ran his thumb-nail over the whorls.

"How did they do it?" he asked again. "Some kind of artificial skin?"

When she lifted a delicate shoulder, he drew back a hand and slapped her across the face. "Stop lying to me!"

She gasped, then met his eyes. "You figure it out."

"I will," he vowed.

BRADY DROVE BACK to La Fontana. After parking in the garage, he took Grace up to his third-floor apartment.

When they stepped inside, he saw her inspecting the place and wondered what she would think of his decor. Although he hadn't paid a lot of attention to fashion details, the furniture was comfortable.

But it seemed she wasn't interested in his decorating skills. Instead she walked to a window and looked out. "We're too high to get out this way."

"We don't have to."

"Are you sure?"

"You think you're in the middle of a conspiracy?"

"I know I'm in the middle of a cover-up. I know Wickers thinks I'm a loose end."

He wanted to argue that this was America, not the Gulag Archipelago. But he remembered his own recent confrontation at gunpoint in the driveway of his brother's estate. Something was going on, and this woman could help him get to the bottom of it. But she was also in trouble, and he was going to keep her safe. At least until he knew the real story.

"You want some coffee?" he asked.

She looked at her watch. "At two in the morning?"

"Well, maybe decaf."

They both walked into the kitchen, where he remembered his previous encounter with his larder.

"Sorry, there's no milk."

"That's okay."

"I forget to buy groceries," he said, wondering why he felt compelled to explain.

"That's okay," she answered again, and he thought from the tone of her voice that perhaps she knew he'd had a wife and daughter—until they'd been killed in a car accident.

Determined to switch the focus back to her, he asked, "You're a freelance researcher?"

"My day job is at the Smithsonian."

"It's a big place. Where exactly?"

"The Air and Space Museum."

"You have an engineering background?"

She laughed. "No. But I can research any subject. I was working on an exhibit that will showcase World War I–era planes. I was recommended to your brother and decided to take the assignment. The autobiography was legit and the pay was good, but I just didn't know I'd also be covering for his…habit."

He ignored the observation as he filled the kettle and set it on a burner. Maybe it was true.

Maybe not. He knew John Ridgeway hadn't been a particularly nice guy. But that was no excuse for murdering him. If it *had* been murder.

"Did you know Karen Hilliard?" he asked. "I mean, outside your contact at the Ridgeway Consortium."

"We knew each other."

"Were you friends?"

"We traveled in some of the same circles," she answered, and he thought she was skating around the truth.

"Which circles?"

"Young DC professionals."

"The bar scene?"

"Sometimes. And parties. Some of them on the Hill. Some at people's houses. Anywhere from basement apartments in Columbia Heights to Georgetown mansions."

"You from DC originally?" he asked her.

She shook her head. "Chicago."

They were standing close together. He could reach out and hold her the way he'd done in the car. To comfort her, he asked himself, or because he wanted to feel her body against his? He wondered if that was the real reason he'd initially decided not to bring her here. Staying in a public place meant he couldn't start anything with her.

He stopped that line of thought. Getting intimate with this woman was the last thing that should be on his mind.

He wondered what she saw in his face when she suddenly said, "You don't have to be tough all the time. It's all right for you to feel...sad about your brother."

"I don't need advice, thanks," he answered quickly, all too aware of the last time he'd let himself give in to grief. But that had been very different. Losing Carol and Lisa had been a body blow. He was still coming to terms with John's passing, but it didn't feel the same. He'd loved his wife and daughter. Fiercely. When he'd learned of John's death, he'd been shocked, but not plunged immediately into a black hole of devastation. He'd miss his brother, but his death wouldn't leave a gaping wound in his life.

"We're not going to talk about me," he added, making his voice firm.

"Why not?"

"It's not relevant."

"You get to make the rules?"

"Yeah. Because I'm the one who drove you away from certain captivity."

"Well, that was very noble of you, but it doesn't mean I can't walk away from you now."

Tension crackled between them. From the look in her eyes, he was sure she would dump him if that suited her plans. He felt a pang he couldn't explain. He wanted to keep her with him, and he didn't even know if it was for the right reasons. For that matter, he didn't know what the right reasons were. He'd started out thinking she was sleeping with his brother. Now he thought she was telling the truth about how she fit into the picture. But the whole truth?

He'd damn well better find out and damn well better keep his head on straight while he did it.

"Where would you go?" he asked.

He was glad to see she looked uncertain. "I haven't thought that far ahead."

"Where were you going when I caught up with you in the alley?"

"Away."

"No specific destination in mind?"

Before she could answer, a knock sounded at the front door.

They both stiffened, and he looked at the clock again. It was just after two. No time for a social visit. Or any kind of visit.

"Maybe you should ask who it is," she whispered.

Yeah, that was the logical first step. He walked toward the door and called out, "Who's there?"

"Ridgeway Security."

He'd smugly assumed that Grace was safe in his apartment. And Grace had been acting as if she didn't need his protection. But when she turned frightened eyes to him, he knew they'd both made major miscalculations.

He kept his voice steady. "Go into the bedroom. It's at the end of the hall."

As she hurried to the back of the apartment, a second knock sounded.

"Just a minute," he called out, rubbing his hand through his hair to muss it up. He walked to the door and looked through the peephole. Through the distorted lens, he saw two tough-looking men standing in the hall. Although it was hard to be sure, he thought he'd never seen either one of them before.

"Open up."

"I'm getting dressed," he answered, undoing the top two buttons of his wrinkled dress shirt.

When he opened the door, the men pushed their way past him and into the apartment.

"Aren't you supposed to ask for permission to enter?" he asked.

"Didn't you just give it to us?"

"No. I want your names."

The one who had been speaking said, "I'm Mosley."

"Kessler," the other one offered.

"Can I see your credentials?"

They both reached inside their suit jackets and brought out small leather cases with their cards and Ridgeway IDs. Unless the creds were fake, both of them worked for his brother's consortium.

"What's this about?" Brady asked as they put the credentials away.

"Your car was spotted in the vicinity of Grace Cunningham's apartment earlier this evening. Is she here?"

He gave the speaker a quizzical look. "I think you're mistaken. Who is Grace Cunningham?"

"She had an appointment with your brother tonight."

"And?"

"Given the untimely demise of Mr. Ridgeway, we want to ask her some questions."

"She's not here."

"Do you mind if we look around?"

"Yes, I mind."

Despite that, Mosley walked past him into the living room. After opening the closet and looking behind the furniture, he searched the kitchen, then started down the hall. Kessler stayed with Brady by the front door, probably so he couldn't escape or make a phone call, Brady guessed.

Brady stared after the man heading for the bedroom. He'd spent a lot of time with his brother, which meant he'd spent a lot of time around his security detail. They always followed procedure, and these guys were acting out of character.

His mind switched from the men to Grace. Had she found a hiding place where the intruder wouldn't discover her?

Unlikely. Unless she'd climbed out the window again. Only, as she'd pointed out, they were too high up for her to find an escape route, unless she also worked as a circus performer or a cat burglar.

He rolled his shoulders, trying to give the impression of fatigue rather than tension.

If they found her here, what the hell was he going to say about it?

He barely knew Grace Cunningham. Yet if she was telling the truth about what had happened this evening at the consortium, he understood why she wanted to avoid falling into the clutches of these men. They'd said they wanted to ask her some questions. She'd said they were in the middle of a cover-up.

"I appreciate your going all out for my brother," Brady said, angling for an opening to... He wasn't sure what. "You seem pretty loyal. How long have you worked for him?"

"How is that relevant?" the man snapped.

"I haven't seen you at the consortium."

"I haven't seen you, either."

Down the hall, Mosley made a grunting sound.

He'd found her. Damn!

Kessler reached into his jacket and pulled out an automatic pistol, then dashed toward the back of the apartment, intent on aiding his partner.

Without making a conscious decision, Brady stuck out his foot and sent the man sprawling. He landed on the wood floor, halfway down the hall.

While the guy was catching his breath, Brady lunged for the desk, grabbed a glass paperweight and brought it down on the back of Kessler's head. He went still.

As he watched blood seep from the man's hair, Brady knew he'd just stepped over an invisible line from harassed citizen protesting a home invasion to criminal. Scrambling over the limp body, he sprinted toward the bedroom.

Mosley was also on the floor—at the side of the bed. He was on top of Grace, trying to wrest his gun from her grasp.

Brady grabbed the man's coat collar and

yanked him backward, just as the gun dis-
charged, the sound reverberating in the con-
fined space.

# Chapter Five

Mosley went rigid. Brady yanked him off of Grace, tucked the gun into the waistband of his own slacks and rolled the man to his back. A bullet hole marred the upper arm of his gray sports jacket. When Brady pulled aside the guy's coat, he saw that a bloodstain had spread across the fabric of his dress shirt. But it was seeping, not pumping from an artery.

Grace pushed herself up off the floor, saw the blood and gasped. "The gun… We." She gulped. "I didn't mean to hit him! I was just trying to keep him from shooting me."

"It's just a flesh wound," Brady answered, wondering if it was true.

Grace's eyes had taken on a glazed look. "I hit him."

The security guy stared at her. "You bitch."

Working methodically, Brady reached for the handcuffs clipped to the back of the man's slacks and cuffed his wrists through the wooden bed frame.

Then he dashed back down the hall. Kessler looked dazed, but he was sitting up and fumbling for the weapon that he'd dropped when he went down.

"No, you don't." Brady grabbed his gun arm and twisted. The man yelped.

"I have your gun. Just don't do anything stupid, and we'll all be okay," he ordered. Raising his voice, he called to Grace, "Get in here."

When she didn't appear, he called her again—more sharply.

She came around the corner of the hall, walking like a drunken sailor, and he knew she was still reacting to the scene with Mosley. And reacting to the knowledge that the whole situation was spinning out of control very quickly.

Did that mean she really was innocent? Regardless, he had to keep her functioning so they could get out of here—because now he was in this as deeply as she.

"His getting shot wasn't your fault," he bit out. "You were fighting for the gun, and it went off."

"In court, that will sound like resisting arrest," she answered, then made a strangled sound when she saw the blood dripping from the other man's head onto the floor.

"Yeah, me too," he muttered. "And they're not cops."

"But they can get us both for assault."

"Maybe they won't want to."

"Why not?"

"Depends on who they really are." He looked at the man on the floor. "Head wounds bleed like a son of a bitch, so it looks worse than it is. Cover him while I make sure he's not going anywhere."

She held the gun in a two-handed grip while he got the guy's cuffs, then helped Kessler to his feet and led him down the hall, where he secured him to the radiator pipe in his office

The security guy glared at him. "You're doing something pretty stupid here. She's in this up to her eyeballs."

"How do you know?"

"She was there."

"But that doesn't make her guilty of anything. She could have been at the wrong place at the wrong time."

"You her lawyer?"

"Something like that. I'll worry about legalities later," he tossed off as he began grabbing items from his desk.

When he was finished, he turned back toward Kessler. "Did Wickers send you?"

Kessler pressed his lips together.

"For what it's worth, I know Wickers is trying to cover up what really happened."

Turning to Grace, he said, "Wait for me in the living room."

She nodded, and he hurried back down the hall. The bloodstain on Mosley's sleeve wasn't much worse, but Brady stopped to grab a tie and make a tourniquet.

The man winced but said nothing.

Returning to Grace, Brady saw she still looked dazed and sounded alarmed when she asked, "What are we going to do?"

"Get out of here."

When she didn't move, he grabbed her arm and hustled her out of the apartment.

She seemed to come back to herself as they hurried down the hall. "Sorry you got caught in the middle of something nasty," she murmured.

"We'll figure it out," he answered, determined to find out what was really going on.

IAN WICKERS SCRUBBED a hand over his face. It felt as if he'd been up for a week of Sundays.

In reality, he was still within his normal workday.

Normal. Yeah, sure.

He bent to the preliminary autopsy report that the DC Police Department had rushed through the system, given the celebrity of the dead man. To Wicker's relief, it confirmed that John Ridgeway had died of a heart attack. At least he wouldn't get caught in a lie over that.

It also listed the drugs in the man's system, with a notation that more might be added to the list after more extensive tests. He recognized them all except one, sildenafil.

When he looked it up, he found it was the active ingredient in Viagra.

Son of a bitch. At least it wasn't illegal. But had Ridgeway been stupid enough to use it when he knew it was contraindicated with the alpha blockers he was taking for his high blood pressure? Or did the woman give it to him without his knowledge? Maybe she'd said it was something else.

He picked up the phone and dialed

Yarborough's pager. A few minutes later, the man appeared in his office.

"How is the interrogation going?" he asked.

"She claims she was hired by Middle Eastern terrorists."

"Is that credible?"

"Maybe."

"What's their motive?"

"She says she doesn't know." The security man shifted his weight from one foot to the other.

"What is it?" Wickers snapped.

"The longer we keep her here, the riskier it gets. I suggest we move her."

"To where?"

"To the facility we have in Northern Virginia."

Wickers weighed the pros and cons. Starting this cover-up had been a knee-jerk reaction to protect John Ridgeway's reputation. Now they were dealing with unanticipated consequences. Like what if the cops wanted to search the Ridgeway Consortium? That would be a little inconvenient if he was keeping a woman captive in the basement.

He sighed and looked up to find Yarborough watching him. "Move her."

BRADY WAS TEMPTED to sprint to the back stairs. Instead he took Grace's arm, and they walked sedately down the hall to the elevator.

"You could have turned me in to those guys," she whispered.

"Would a bodyguard turn in the woman he's guarding?"

"You're serious about that?"

"Yeah," he answered, still not sure which way this whole thing was going to go. Or was he already in too deep to get back on the right side of the law? Until a few minutes ago, he hadn't done anything illegal. Then his instincts had taken over.

"Thanks," she murmured. When they reached the basement level, she said, "They already spotted your car once. They'll be on the lookout for it again."

"I won't be driving anything they'll recognize."

Her head snapped up. "What are you going to do—steal some wheels from one of your neighbors?"

"No. I have several vehicles down here—for undercover assignments." He mentally considered his choices and decided on a gray Ford. The body had seen better days, but the engine was in excellent condition.

They strolled into the garage as if she was his houseguest and they were going out for groceries. But when he looked at her pale face, he couldn't stop himself from pulling her into his arms.

She clung to him, and he held her tightly.

"You feel better?" he asked her.

"No, but at least we got out of there."

He nodded, but he knew in his gut that there was more to come. They'd be looking for him and Grace.

He eased away—it was dangerous to linger in the garage.

He led her to the car he'd selected.

"Get in the back—and lie on the seat—so it looks like there's just one person in the car."

"Okay."

When she was settled, he reached into the carry bag he'd brought, took out a baseball cap and pulled it low over his face before heading for the automatic garage door. The gears ground, and he waited an eternity for the door to open. Finally, he drove into the night, a fugitive from the law. Or would the two security men report what had happened to the cops?

He drove for about twenty minutes before he looked over his shoulder to see Grace lying on her side on the backseat, hugging her knees against her middle.

"I think it's safe for you to get in the front now."

"Thanks."

He pulled onto a side street and stopped.

As she climbed into the front seat, she asked, "Do you think those men are really from the Ridgeway Consortium?"

"Why do you ask?"

"They don't seem much like the guards I've seen there. What if they work for someone else?"

"Who?"

She shrugged, but he wondered if she might have an idea about their identity.

"No idea?" he pressed.

"No."

"What happened in the bedroom before I got there?" he asked, changing the subject abruptly.

She swallowed hard. "That guy came in and started looking around. I was in the closet. I knew he was going to find me there, so I waited until his back was turned and jumped him."

"Risky."

"What would you have done?"

"The same."

She laughed. "At least I feel better about my decision."

"Don't use me as a shining example of anything."

"Don't run yourself down," she shot back.

When he didn't come back with a rejoinder, she looked out the window into the darkness. "Where are we going?"

"Hell if I know. I haven't gotten that far yet."

"Can I make a suggestion?"

"I thought you didn't have any plans when you escaped from your apartment."

"I didn't have a car. But now that we do, I know of an unoccupied cabin in the Catoctin Mountains."

"Up by Camp David?"

She nodded.

"Perfect. There's a lot of security up there."

"A good reason to assume you won't go in that direction."

"Who owns the cabin?"

"Friends," she answered quickly. "But they don't use it at this time of year."

"Some of your young DC professionals?"

Again she paused. "Yes."

"Are you leading me into a trap?"

"No."

He waited a beat before bringing up another touchy subject. "You realize we can't just leave two wounded men in my apartment."

She swallowed. "Yes."

IT WAS EARLY in the morning, but Washington was a city where traffic never stopped.

Phil Yarborough sat in the passenger seat of the unmarked white van as it traveled along the toll road to Reston, Virginia. When he felt the driver's foot bounce on the accelerator, he looked over inquiringly.

"What?"

"Two patrol cars are closing in on us with their lights flashing. What do I do now?"

"You're not exceeding the speed limit?"

"Of course not!" the driver snapped.

"And you don't think you have a taillight out—or anything like that?"

"This vehicle was checked before we left the Ridgeway Consortium."

"Better pull over."

The van slowed, then swung onto the shoulder. One patrol car stopped in back of the vehicle. The other boxed them in front.

Yarborough watched as two uniformed officers got out of each vehicle. Lord, now what?

As they walked toward the driver's door, he rolled down his window.

One of the officers pulled some papers from his jacket pocket. "This is authorization to transfer your prisoner."

"What authorization?" Yarborough snapped. Reaching across the driver, he held out his hand.

The officer gave him the papers and he found he was reading a federal court order transferring custody of Karen Hilliard to the Justice Department.

"The orders comes from the Department of Homeland Security, under the Patriot Act," the officer clarified.

Yarborough cursed under his breath. Somehow that Middle Eastern terrorist story had gotten out.

"Why wasn't I informed of this?" he asked.

"I guess the authorization just came through."

"I need to call my boss." Yarborough wasn't happy.

## Chapter Six

The officer gave Yarborough a look that he himself had used on many occasions. It said that the cop held all the cards in this game.

"You can talk to him later. Right now, we want the prisoner," he said, his hand on his hip, dangling inches from his sidearm.

The voice and the gesture weren't lost on Yarborough. "Why is the Justice Department using local cops?"

"We were in the area."

Yarborough didn't like it. But he didn't see himself getting into a gun battle on the highway shoulder—with the cops. That would be a little tough to explain.

He climbed out, then walked around to the back of the van and unlocked the door. Karen Hilliard sat on a bench seat, her hands cuffed to a ring on the metal bar beside her seat, her legs shackled to keep her steps slow and labored.

She looked from him to the uniforms.

"What's happening?" she asked.

"Change of custody. It sounds like the Department of Homeland Security is getting into the act."

"How?"

"Damned if I know."

She look frightened as he detached her cuffs.

"Don't let them take me," she whispered.

"I don't have any choice."

"Please."

He'd been pretty tough on her, and she wanted to stay with him? That was almost enough to make him protest. But he knew he wasn't going to get anywhere.

One of the uniforms grabbed her arm and helped her up, then escorted her from the van toward a patrol car.

Yarborough followed, and the cop whirled. "Can I do something for you?"

"Sign a receipt for the prisoner."

"Certainly."

Yarborough wrote out a note saying that the officer had removed Karen Hilliard from Ridgeway Security custody.

The man signed his name—Burton Temple.

When he turned and climbed back into the patrol car, there was nothing Yarborough could do besides watch him drive away.

BRADY WAITED UNTIL he'd driven into Maryland and was heading up Route 270, against the traffic flowing into town. Taking one hand from the wheel, he pulled his cell phone from the clip on his belt. "I'm going to call Ridgeway Security."

Grace made a gulping sound. "You have to?"

"You know I do."

She sighed, and he took that for agreement.

He brought up his phone directory, then scrolled to the "R" section.

When a male voice answered, he identified himself. "This is Brady Lockwood. Do you have two men named Mosley and Kessler in that office?"

"Yes."

Feeling his breath turn shallow, he asked, "May I speak to one of them?"

"Just a moment."

His hand tightened on the phone as he waited. Beside him, he could see Grace's rigid profile.

Then a voice came on the line. "Mosley."

"You're with the Ridgeway Consortium Security detail?"

"Yes."

"This is Brady Lockwood. Did you show up at my apartment in La Fontana this evening?"

"Negative."

Brady turned his head toward Grace and saw that she had heard the man's answer.

"Well, two guys impersonating you and Agent Kessler are at my place."

"Where are you now?"

"Not at home."

"I'd like your location."

"Sorry. Maybe if you hustle over to my place, you can catch the impostors and ask what they were up to."

Before Mosley could ask any more questions, Brady ended the call and turned off the phone.

Grace breathed out a sigh, then turned her head toward him. "I guess we have confirmation that they weren't legit."

"Unless Wickers is running some kind of scam."

"Why would he?"

Brady shrugged. "Because nothing's making a whole lot of sense."

Grace nodded. "What made you suspect them?"

"They were too pushy."

"So I shot some sort of impostor—not somebody official."

"Right."

She leaned back and closed her eyes for a moment. "That's something, anyway."

"Who were they?" he asked.

Her head whipped toward him. "You expect me to know?"

"They were looking for you. And a few hours ago, men showed up at your house. Are these the same guys?"

She considered for a moment. "I...don't think so. And maybe they weren't really after me. Maybe they were using me as an excuse to get into your apartment." Even as she proposed the theory, she didn't sound entirely confident.

"You don't have any clues about who they are?" he pressed.

"No!" She put force behind the denial. But

he watched her take her lower lip between her teeth.

"Maybe you should trust me," he said.

"I want to."

He studied her tight expression, knowing that statement only went so far. She had accepted his bodyguard role, but she still hadn't come clean with him.

He was almost sure that even if she wasn't the woman with his brother when he died, she knew more than she was admitting.

"But you're not giving me all the facts," he said and watched her look down at her hands, hiding her expression from him.


PHIL YARBOROUGH pressed the speed dial on his phone.

Wickers answered on the second ring. "You've got her stashed at the safe house?"

"No."

"What do you mean 'no'?"

"A couple of cop cars stopped us and then hustled her away."

"Why didn't you stop them?"

"Stop armed police officers?"

"What jurisdiction?"

"Fairfax County."

"Okay. Stay in your car. I'll find out what's going on."

GRACE STARED THROUGH the windshield, thinking that she'd gotten herself and Brady Lockwood into a hell of a mess. He'd asked if she had any idea why two guys posing as Ridgeway Security men would come after her. She suspected they worked for a man who called himself the Paladin. But she couldn't tell that to Brady—because then she'd have a lot more to explain.

"So your friends don't mind your using their cabin?" Brady asked.

She knit her fingers together in her lap. Although she'd said she was from Chicago, that had been a lie. She was from this area, and the cabin belonged to her parents, but they were never there around this time of the year—except on weekends. Now she wished she'd just kept her mouth shut and let him suggest something.

Mom and Dad. Ellen and Stan Cutler. Not Cunningham. That was the name she'd taken after she'd known she had to disappear.

They'd been so good to her, so grateful to have a baby, and she couldn't imagine a more loving childhood. They'd given her every opportunity—from gymnastics classes to piano lessons. She'd gone to a private school and then to one of the country's top colleges. And how had she repaid them? By breaking their hearts.

She turned her head toward the side window, letting Brady know that she didn't want to be drawn into a conversation. But he didn't take the hint.

"How did you get the job working for my brother? I mean, how did he find you?"

"I was introduced to him at a party, and he asked about my background."

"Which is?"

"I have a B.A. in history from Barnard and a Masters from the George Washington University," she answered, giving him her fake background.

"He doesn't usually hire women he meets at parties."

"Well, a week after your brother and I met, I got a call from someone at the Ridgeway Consortium asking if I'd like a part-time job. Naturally, I was flattered."

"Naturally."

"It didn't take me long to figure out that he was using our meetings as an excuse to slip away and see Karen Hilliard."

"Why didn't you quit?"

Grace raised her chin. "You don't just quit a job with a powerful man in Washington. I have the feeling you understand that pretty well. You didn't like everything your brother asked you to do for him, did you?"

"No."

She saw his hands tighten on the wheel.

She was about to make the point by asking

what kind of jobs he'd taken for his brother when a tinny rendition of Beethoven's "Ode to Joy" interrupted her.

"My phone," she exclaimed and scrambled in her purse.

"Who is it?" Brady asked.

She flipped the phone open and peered at the screen. "Not a number I recognize. It's in Maryland."

"Answer it."

A shiver traveled over her skin. "What if it's those guys?"

"Ask them how they got your number—before we pitch the phone out the window."

She pressed the talk button. "Hello?"

"Thank God," a woman's voice said.

"Karen?" She threw a quick glance at Brady, who raised an eyebrow, then turned his head back toward the highway.

The voice on the other end of the line hitched. "Yes."

"Where are you?"

"I got away."

"How?"

"Some people helped me."

"Who?"

"I don't want to get into anything over the phone."

"Where are you?"

"At a house I own in Frederick. Can you meet me there?"

When she hesitated, Karen went on quickly. "I know you don't like me."

"Not you. What you're doing."

"Put that aside. I need to talk to you."

"I—"

Before Grace could respond, Brady lifted the phone out of her hand. "This is Brady Lockwood," he said in a hard voice. "Who is this?"

The volume was loud, and he assumed Grace could hear both sides of the conversation, the way he'd been able to.

"You're with Grace?" Karen asked.

"Yes. Who is this?" he demanded again.

"Karen Hilliard."

He glanced at Grace, then back at the road. "How did you get this number?"

"I know that Ridgeway was using Grace. We…talked, and exchanged numbers. I need her help now. I think Wickers is trying make it look like I killed your brother."

"You know who I am?"

"Yes."

"You're saying you're not involved in my brother's death?"

"Yes."

"But you were having an affair with him."

He heard her swallow hard. "Yes."

"Why should I believe anything you say?"

"I'll answer any question you ask, but not on the phone. Please meet me in Frederick. I'm at a house out on Snyder Road." She went on to give an address. He repeated it to make sure Grace got it as she pulled out a pen and paper.

"Please hurry." Before Brady could reply, the phone clicked off.

He slowed the car and pulled to the shoulder

of the road, where he turned to face Grace, feeling his features stiffen.

"All right, tell me what the hell is going on? Was that really Karen Hilliard?"

"I think so."

"And how did the two of you get to be pals? I mean—really."

"We're not pals! When I found out what she was up to, I confronted her."

He kept the conversation going. "You said you knew her."

"She told me if she got into trouble, I could, too."

He closed his hand over her shoulder. "Even though you were an innocent bystander?"

"Yes. And it looks like she was right. Guys have been coming after me since this happened."

His hand tightened on her shoulder. "I think you have a better idea about what's going on than I do."

"I wish I did."

He studied her face. "And why did Hilliard call you now?"

"She said she wants my help."

"Why should you give it to her?"

Grace swallowed. "Because I got the feeling she'd been trapped into something she didn't like—that she was in over her head."

"You think she murdered my brother?"

"We can ask her."

Brady snorted. "Oh sure. Why should she tell me anything? Or have the two of you cooked up some story you're planning to feed me?"

In the face of the accusation, Grace's face turned ashen. "I haven't talked to her since I escaped from the Ridgeway Consortium. How could I have cooked something up with her?"

"You tell me."

## Chapter Seven

Brady watched Grace swallow hard. "I'm not lying. I don't approve of what she did."

"Which was what—exactly?"

"Having an affair with a married man. A powerful man who could maybe…help her."

"That's all?"

She pressed her lips together.

"You think she's involved in some kind of conspiracy? That she caused his death?"

She gave one of her maddening little shrugs. "Maybe she's desperate enough to play it straight with us."

"Us," he said, clipping out the syllable.

"Yeah, sure. Us. I could drop you in Frederick, and you could take a cab to her place."

Panic leaped in her eyes. "What about the… bodyguard thing?"

"What about it?"

"I thought I could go it alone. But we both know I'm already in over my head," she said in a low voice. "Somebody wants to make sure I don't talk about what I've seen and heard."

"I thought you said you could walk away from me."

"That was before those men showed up at your apartment."

"Maybe they just wanted you for questioning."

"You believe that?"

"No," he answered, weighing the pros and cons of letting her drag him into the swamp with her.

Something was going on. Something he didn't understand. If Grace Cunningham didn't know what it was, she had her suspicions. He'd started off wanting to know what had really happened to his brother. Now he was starting to think that John Ridgeway might be only one piece in a complicated puzzle, and maybe this meeting was the best chance to get some answers.

"All right," Brady sighed and watched her let out the breath she'd been holding. He pulled back onto the road, then exited and turned around, heading for Frederick instead of the Camp David area.

They were only an hour from Frederick. Was that a coincidence? Did Grace suspect that they'd be heading in this direction? Or was he reading extra meaning into everything that happened?

He spared her a quick glance. She was sitting rigidly in her seat, her hands twined in a death grip.

"You know where to find Karen's house?"

"I've never been there. I assume we can get directions."

He drove for another quarter mile, then said,

"Give me some background. I want to know more about you."

"Why?"

"So I can get a good feel for whether you're lying."

"Nice."

"Start talking. Where did you grow up? I don't mean a vague nod to Chicago. What part? What high school did you go to? What kind of grocery story did your mom patronize."

She looked as if she was having a silent debate with herself. Finally she said, "Okay. Not Chicago."

He made a rough sound. "Why did you tell me a story?"

"I didn't know you very well. I didn't want to get my family involved."

That might make sense—in a strange sort of way.

"So now that you know me better, where did you grow up?"

She sighed. "I'm from the Silver Spring area. I went to Montgomery Blair High School. My dad worked for the Maryland state government. My mom taught elementary school. They gave me a good home."

"That's a strange way to put it." He wished they were somewhere else besides the car—where he could watch her eyes when she answered his questions. She was speaking carefully. So—was she lying? Or shading the truth? Apparently she still didn't know him well enough to be straight with him.

Her next statement took him by surprise.

"I was adopted. They really wanted a baby, so they worked through a lawyer to get me. I think they used some money they'd inherited from an aunt of Mom's."

"Did you ever try to contact your birth mother?"

She hesitated for a moment.

"That's not a difficult question."

"I tried. I didn't get anywhere. The records were sealed."

"So you had a good childhood?"

"Yes. Did you?" she asked, turning the tables

on him. "I know your mom divorced Mr. Ridgeway. Then later married your father."

"Well, actually, he divorced her. It was nine years before she met my father. That's why there's eighteen years difference between me and John. And why he had more...privileges than I did."

"His father was wealthy?"

"Yes. John inherited a substantial trust fund. I had to work for a living. I was good in math. Good with electronics. I went to a community college—then the University of Maryland. I had college loans. And I borrowed money to start my computer-repair business. From there I got a job with the Light Street Detective Agency. I still did computer work, but I became interested in some of their investigations—and they brought me into that end of the business."

When he realized he'd volunteered a lot of information, he stopped talking abruptly.

"You're leaving stuff out," she said.

"Like what?"

"Your wife and daughter died," she finished.

His hands gripped the wheel. "You know about that? What did you do, research me?"

"No. I already told you, I was researching Ridgeway, at his request." She paused. "And he used to talk about you. He said you did a lot of work for him. He said he got you back on your feet after you…"

"After I drank myself into oblivion," he finished.

"You don't have to put it that way."

"How would *you* put it?"

"You were self-medicating."

He snorted. "You know the phrase—recovering alcoholic. Some bodyguard. I could crap out on you at any time."

"You won't."

"How do you know?"

"You said you stopped by your brother's house. You didn't join his wife in a drink when you found out about John's death."

"How do you know Lydia had a drink?"

"I'm making assumptions, based on what her husband said about her."

"Which is what?"

"She was an aristocrat. She had connections that opened doors for him. But he was disappointed that she didn't want children. And he was disappointed that she started drinking in the afternoons when she was bored."

"Yeah. That's pretty accurate."

He watched her. She knew a hell of a lot more about him and his family than he knew about her. But one thing he did understand. She was withholding information. He wanted to demand that she come clean with him. But he suspected that would be a waste of time.

IAN WICKERS MANAGED to keep from slamming down the phone. Pulling out his pocket handkerchief, he wiped a film of perspiration from his forehead, then replaced the white linen square in his pocket.

It had taken some time to get through to the Chief of Police in Fairfax County. But as far as the chief knew, none of his officers had taken a prisoner away from Ridgeway Security.

Which had led to a couple of questions that Wickers didn't want to answer. So he'd pulled rank with some National Security bullshit.

He'd thought about calling some of the other jurisdictions in the area. But if they didn't have Karen Hilliard, then he'd have to go through the same story again, and he was willing to bet his Ridgeway pension that Yarborough hadn't made a mistake about the name of the jurisdiction on the cop car. The man might be a son of a bitch, but he was no fool. He knew exactly what was involved. And he wouldn't have let Officer Burton Temple take the prisoner unless he'd been shoved into a corner.

The problem now was that the Fairfax County Police didn't have an officer named Burton Temple. But somebody had taken Karen Hilliard away from Yarborough. Who the hell was that? And that wasn't his only problem. Patrick Frazier, the pushy deputy chief of Ridgeway Consortium, wanted to be confirmed as the next CEO of the consortium as soon as possible. Or, more likely, it was that bitch of a wife of his, Barbara Frazier, who was doing the insisting. Barbara was ambitious for her husband, more ambitious than he was for himself.

AS THEY REACHED the outskirts of Frederick, Brady wished he'd thought to bring his computer when they'd bailed out of La Fontana. He could have gone to a hot spot and called up Mapquest to get directions. Instead, he stopped at a gas station and filled his tank.

When Grace saw him start to slide the card into the credit slot, she jumped out of the car and grabbed his arm.

"Don't!"

The touch of her chilled fingers against his skin made him go still.

"They can track you through your transactions."

He gave her what he hoped was a cocky grin. "They could—if it were in my name."

He held up the plastic rectangle for her inspection—so she could see the name Barry Logan in the front.

"I acquired the identity a couple of years ago when I was working for the Light Street Detective Agency. I use it when I don't want to reveal my real name."

"Handy. If you're on the lam."

The way she said it made him wonder if she knew more about the subject than she was saying.

After paying for the gas, he bought one of those rectangular maps that never folded back up the way they came. On it he located Snyder Road, which turned out to be a country lane east of the city and about fifteen minutes from where they were.

He found the number on the mailbox and slowed. The house was in the middle of a scraggly field, up a narrow, rutted lane, and he didn't particularly like the setup. The structure was old and weathered, with faded gray shingles and peeling white paint on the door and window frames. A detached garage had once stood in back of the house, but it had collapsed and lay in an untidy heap in the backyard.

Beside him, Grace was sitting rigidly, staring at the sagging residence.

"Have you ever been here before?" he asked.

"No."

"Does it look like the kind of place where a woman who attracted my brother would live?"

She took her lower lip between her teeth, then released it. "No. She's too classy for a place like this."

"Even as a hideout?"

"Maybe not."

He gave Grace a sharp look. "Are you sure that was her on the phone?"

"Yes."

Instead of stopping, he kept going past the house.

"What are you doing? We have to..." Grace's voice was high and strained.

"Check out the area," he finished for her.

The next house was at least a seventy-five yards away. He saw a car parked in front of it and a woman hanging laundry on a line outside.

After driving about a half mile, he turned around and started back, scanning the fields on either side of the road. Grace was doing the same.

At least he didn't see anyone hiding in the weeds.

Maybe they were in the stand of woods a hundred yards away, waiting for him and Grace to go into the house.

He turned to her. "You're determined to go in there?"

"I don't think I have a choice."

"There's always a choice."

She huffed out a breath. "Okay, I *want* to do it."

Of course, he didn't have to go with her. But he wasn't going to leave her unprotected. "Stay close to me," he said as he pulled into the gravel parking area, reversing the direction of the car so that it was pointed down the driveway.

"If there's trouble, we're getting out of here fast," he said firmly.

"What about Karen?"

"We don't even know if she's in there."

He pulled the gun from where he'd set it on the floor before climbing out and inspecting the area.

Grace had also climbed out, and he motioned for her to follow him to the front door.

When he knocked on the door, he thought he heard a voice within, but nobody appeared.

Pushing the door open, he stepped into a living room that was furnished with the kind of ugly orange-stained maple furniture that had been popular fifty years earlier.

When he heard a noise from down the hallway, he froze. It sounded like a groan or a plea.

Despite his instructions and Grace's earlier agreement to stay close to him, she darted into the hall, then into a bedroom where he saw an ornate brass bed.

A woman was lying on it, one of her hands chained to the brass rail above her head. Her black dress was pulled up around her hips, and she wore no panties.

Grace gasped. "Karen! What happened? Were you raped? What?"

Brady followed Grace into the room.

"Help me," the woman on the bed begged, her voice slurred as she clawed at something on the arm that was shackled to the bed.

Grace drew in a sharp breath as she ran forward, leaning over to pull down the woman's skirt while Brady studied her. She must have been good-looking and well-groomed to have attracted John Ridgeway, but now her ash-blond hair was matted, her blue eyes were bloodshot and her pale skin was splotched.

She'd sounded coherent when he talked to her on the phone an hour ago. Now she looked dazed. She was drugged, sick or injured. Or all three.

"What happened to you?" he asked. Had she been sexually assaulted, or did someone want to make it look that way—to distract them from what was really going on?

She blinked, trying to focus her blue eyes on him. As he stared into those eyes, he went still. He'd seen her before. No, he'd remember her. He was sure of it. He'd never met her before. Had he?

"What happened to you?" he repeated, his tone demanding answers.

Once again, she clawed at her arm, her fingernails digging a hole in her blouse. Below the fabric he could make out some kind of mark on her skin, but he couldn't see what it was.

Grace sat on the edge of the bed, leaning over to stroke the other woman's hair back from her face.

Karen blinked. "Grace, what are you doing here?"

"You called me."

"Did I?"

"Yes. Tell me what happened to you."

The woman on the bed only shook her head.

"She's in bad shape."

"Yeah." He switched his attention back to the blonde. "Focus! What happened?"

"They took me…" she said vaguely, her voice trailing off.

Grace sat down on the bed and pulled ineffectively at the handcuff. "Who? Who took you?"

"Don't know. Maybe the Pal…" Again she failed to finish the sentence.

Grace gasped, then turned pleadingly to Brady. "We have to get her out of here. She needs a doctor. And whoever handcuffed her could be coming back."

"Yeah."

He needed information. "Where did you meet Ridgeway?" he asked.

She licked her lips.

"Where?"

Once again, she made an effort to focus on him. "Party..."

"Whose party?"

"Bar..."

"You were paid to seduce John Ridgeway?"

"Yes."

"By whom?"

"Terrorists."

"From where?"

She gave him a vague look.

"For God's sake, you can't interrogate her now," Grace interjected. "We've got to get her out of here. See if there's something you can use to cut the chain on the handcuff."

He started out of the room, then looked back to see Grace leaning over the captive, talking soothingly to her. Karen was thrusting her head toward her left arm, making sounds that Brady couldn't hear.

He'd like to know what she was trying to say. He'd like to know what the two women were to each other because it sure looked as if they were more than casual acquaintances.

Maybe whoever had chained Karen up had given her a hallucinogen, and she wasn't even in touch with reality.

He wanted to get the hell out of the house. But he wasn't going to leave the woman there, chained up like the victim in a sadomasochistic movie.

"Be right back."

In the kitchen he began rifling through drawers. He found some ragged towels and old knives and forks. Nothing that looked as if it was going to cut through the handcuff chain. Maybe it would be easier to take the rails of the brass bed apart. Perhaps he could use a rock from outside.

Grace came running back down the hall. "There's something wrong with her. I think she's having a convulsion."

"We'll get her to the hospital."

He had just opened the kitchen door and started back down the hall with Grace when an explosion shook the house, and they were thrown to the floor. As debris rained down from the back of the house, they both started coughing.

Sitting up, he looked at the destruction around them.

Grace also pushed herself to a sitting position. Her dark hair was covered with plaster dust. "Brady. Oh God, Brady, what happened?"

"A bomb," he answered, just as fire sprang up from the bedroom. The bomb must have gone off right next to Karen Hilliard—right where they'd both been a few moments ago.

Flames sprang up in the hall.

"Get back." He took Grace's hand and pulled her away from the fire.

"We have to get her out of there," Grace gasped, her eyes wide with panic.

Could they?

He dragged a struggling Grace to the kitchen sink. To his relief, it worked. As cold water gushed out of the faucet he soaked three of the towels. Wrapping them around himself, he ran down the corridor again, but he couldn't make it past the flames.

When he saw the bed engulfed by the fire, he knew there was no way Karen had survived. They'd lucked out by going into the kitchen. Otherwise they'd be cooked, too.

When Grace tried to run past him, he grabbed her. "No! She's dead."

Grace moaned.

The fire was eating its way toward them, and he knew they had to get out of the house before it was too late. "Come on."

When Grace resisted, he grabbed her arm and led her toward the back door.

"No. Please," she gasped. "Help me. We've got to get her out of here."

He saw she couldn't wrap her head around the truth. "I'm sorry. It's too late. Nobody could survive in there."

She looked back toward the burning bedroom, and he saw tears in her eyes. He didn't know whether they were caused by her emotions or by the smoke that was billowing around them.

"Get down where there's more oxygen," he told her.

When Grace resisted, he pulled her toward the floor, and she came down beside him on her hands and knees. At the floor level, it was easier to breathe.

"This way."

Coughing, he led her toward the front door, which was the only way they could go without running into the flames that were creeping toward them.

They were both choking when he reached the front door, reached up to grab the knob and turned it.

He was about to step outside when a bullet slammed into the front door, inches from his face.

## Chapter Eight

Brady returned fire, then jumped back, slamming the door behind him.

"Someone's shooting?" Grace gasped.

"Yeah. Stay down."

She pressed herself against the floor, coughing. "What are we going to do?"

He looked around. Through the smoke, he saw there were windows on either side of the living room.

The fire crackled in the hall, creeping closer to them, and he wondered whether they were going to get broiled or shot.

"This way. The window on the left," he

gasped, crawling across the floor, then stopping to make sure Grace was behind him.

When they reached the side of the room, he bashed the butt of his gun against the windowpane.

The fire had made it to the end of the living room, and they were both breathing hard when he broke the window, then kicked the glass out of the way.

"I'm going to lay down a…burst of…fire. Run…for the woods…" he told Grace. She was about to climb out the window, when he saw a gunman coming around the side of the house.

His low curse was followed by a coughing fit. When he fired, the guy jumped back, but he knew that his head was getting muzzy and his aim was off.

"Stay here," he managed to gasp out.

"We can't."

"I'll go out shooting. You follow me."

"You'll get hit."

"Got a better suggestion?"

Before she could answer the question, he heard a siren coming rapidly toward them.

The fire department. Maybe the cops. Silently he thanked the neighbor lady for calling 911.

The man closing in on them hesitated, then touched his ear, and Brady knew he was listening to directions.

When the gunman backed up and disappeared into the woods, Brady let out the breath he was holding. Still, he didn't know if the first person out the window would get nailed.

But one thing was certain: the fire was licking relentlessly across the floor toward them and up the walls. Next the ceiling was going to come down on them or the floor would give way.

Throwing a sofa cushion onto the sill to shield himself from the glass, he climbed out the window, then breathed a sigh of relief when he didn't feel a bullet slam into him.

"Come on."

Grace leaned out, and he grasped her around the waist and lifted her down. He could

already see a fire truck coming up the driveway. Making a split-second decision, he wiped
his gun off on the tail of his shirt and tossed it
into the weeds.

"What are you doing?"

"Getting caught with a weapon isn't the best
strategy at the moment."

Both of them staggered into the front yard,
just as a fire engine pulled up in front of the
house and men in protective gear piled out. His
impulse was to get the hell out of there, but in
this case, he figured the authorities were the
better choice.

Taking Grace's hand, he stepped toward the
fireman. The one in the lead took in the soot
and plaster dust clinging to their clothing.

"What happened?"

"An explosion," Brady answered. "I don't
know from what, though."

"You live here?"

He shook his head. "We came to visit a
friend."

"An ambulance is on the way."

"We're okay," Grace said, her voice raspy.

Brady put a hand on her arm. "I think we should be checked out."

She gave him a questioning look, but when he shook his head, she clamped her lips shut.

As the firefighter joined the rest of the crew, Brady turned to Grace. "The safest way to get out of here is to let them take us to the hospital."

She nodded.

"Are you okay?"

Her face looked stark. "Yes, but…"

"There was nothing you could do for Karen. That bomb went off right beside her."

"I'm trying to come to grips with that." She gave him a sick look. "The police will see she was handcuffed to the bedpost."

He nodded.

"They meant to kill her."

"And us. They lured us here."

"Lured me."

"They knew you were with me. I think it's a twofer."

CHARLES HANCOCK didn't like to keep any set schedule. He was actually due to fly to his farm in upstate New York, but the current crisis had changed his plans. He was still in the DC area where he could keep his finger on the pulse of the operation. For all the good that was doing him. Had something gone wrong at the house in Frederick?

Reaching for the remote, he turned on the television, but there was no local news at the moment. And the cable networks were all wound up with the president's latest speech on the war. As if talking about it was going to fix the problem.

Unable to sit still, he climbed off the leather couch and walked to the window, where he stood staring out at his koi pond and the land-scaped acreage beyond. An artificial stream flowed into the pond, which was edged with natural rocks. It was all so well done that you could believe you were in a wilderness. At this time of day, the sun made a harsh glare on the water—fitting his mood.

When the phone rang, he spun away from the window and strode across the room. Snatching up the instrument, he asked, "Well?"

There was a pause on the other end of the line.

"It was a partial success."

"Partial?" he asked, hearing the dangerous edge in his own voice.

"Karen Hilliard is dead. Lockwood and Cunningham got away."

"Why?"

"The bomb must have been defective. It didn't kill them in the initial blast."

Hancock fought not to swear. He'd always believed that if you wanted something done right, you had to do it yourself. Yet there were jobs he couldn't take on personally.

"They were inside the house. We had them pinned down, and they would have burned up in there, but the fire department arrived. We had to leave."

Struggling to control his anger, he asked, "Where are they now?"

"The fire department is here. I assume an ambulance will take them to the hospital."

"Then go to the hospital and scoop them up. They're a danger to us. They have to be eliminated."

BRADY STEADIED GRACE as he stated the obvious. "You do know that when they find a woman chained to the bed, they're going to think we're the ones who put her there."

Grace gasped.

"We're the only ones here, which makes us the chief suspects. And I'll bet they're not going to find any fingerprints inside the house besides ours—if there are any left to find."

The conversation was interrupted by the arrival of the ambulance.

EMTs hurried toward them.

The lead man looked at the burning house. "How long were you in there after the fire started?"

It had seemed like centuries. "Probably only a couple of minutes."

"I'd advise lying down while we check you out," one of the medics said.

Brady wanted to stay on his feet, but he figured that the more he acted like a normal victim, the better. So he and Grace eased onto stretchers, then were fitted with oxygen masks.

As one of the men gave him a quick examination, Brady's mind went back over what had happened at the house before the explosion. From the way they'd interacted, he'd swear that Grace and Karen knew each other pretty well, and he was going to make her explain what was going on. As soon as they were alone again.

He and Grace were wheeled to the ambulance for the ride to the emergency room. He'd told Grace that the ambulance was the best way to escape the fire scene. As soon as they arrived at the hospital, they had other problems.

Before anybody could ask for identification or insurance information, he moved to Grace's side.

"Come on."

"Where are we going?"

"Away."

"They said they were going to check us for carbon monoxide and hydrogen cyanide poisoning."

"I guess we're going to have to take a chance on that. I'm going to call a cab," he told her.

He eased the door open and stepped out. As he walked toward the front of the waiting area, he saw a tough-looking man enter the E.R. He recognized him as the shooter who'd tried to keep him pinned down in the burning house. And Brady was pretty sure he hadn't come here to get a splinter removed.

His heart pounded as the guy crossed the patient area, headed for the exam rooms.

A nurse stopped him. "Can I help you?"

"I'm looking for my sister. I dropped her off an hour ago, and she hasn't come home."

"You'll have to wait in the front."

The man looked annoyed, but he stepped back to the seating area.

Turning, Brady hurried back the way he'd come. When he looked for Grace, she was gone.

Panic surged inside him. Had another one of the thugs already scooped her up?

Then he saw her emerge from the ladies' room, putting her phone back into her purse.

Who the hell had she called?

Someone who had sent the goon he'd just seen? It didn't seem likely, but he couldn't discount the possibility that she'd set the ambush up somehow. But she'd almost gotten killed. Maybe her friends had double-crossed her.

And maybe he should just leave her here.

That might be the most logical course of action, but the idea made his stomach muscles knot. He wasn't going to leave her. Unless he had solid evidence that she'd set him up.

Reaching her, he said in a low voice, "Keep going. Toward the back." At her questioning look, he explained, "One of our friends from the house has followed us here."

She sucked in a sharp breath and let him

lead her away from the entrance. "What are we going to do?"

"I'm thinking."

He wished he knew the layout of the hospital. They'd come in through the ambulance door, but he was sure the bad guys had covered that escape route.

There were offices along the hall, but none of them had windows. Finally they came to a storage room.

Brady looked around and saw shelves with packages of scrub suits and other supplies.

"In here."

He turned on the light and gestured toward the hospital garb. "Put some of those over your clothing."

She touched his face. "You're covered with soot."

"Damn."

"Try to brush off your clothes."

He unwrapped a scrub suit and used it as a rag to dust himself. Grace did the same. Then she picked up a bottle of water and poured some on another set of scrubs. She dabbed at his face until the soot washed off.

"You too," he said as he took more scrubs from the shelf. He was fairly successful cleaning her up.

"How do I look?" she asked in a quavery voice.

The way she struggled to hold her voice steady undid him.

"Grace..."

He pulled her into his arms, and they clung together, like two survivors of a shipwreck who had finally washed up on solid ground. Only it was an unknown island, and neither one of them knew what dangers lurked in the lush green jungle that started where the sand ended.

He barely knew her. He didn't trust her. He should ease away from her before it was too late.

Too late for what? To get involved? They were already involved in ways he couldn't spell out, and he found himself tightening his embrace, aware of every sweet curve of her body—her breasts, the feminine roundness of her hips, the indentation at her waist.

Leaning forward, he pressed his lips to hers. Instant heat flared between them. They'd just survived certain death. And the power of that realization was as much to blame as anything else.

They were alive. And, at least at that moment, the experience had bonded them.

His lips moved over hers, urgently and none too gently. But she didn't pull away. Instead, she leaned into him, her mouth warm and welcoming.

She opened for him, and his tongue swept into her mouth, claiming her with a passion that shocked him. It had been a long time since he'd kissed a woman—wanted a woman—but need flared white-hot inside him.

He pulled her closer, lowering his hands to her bottom, his hips moving urgently against hers. He had stopped thinking about anything besides the woman in his arms and the way she was responding to him. Mutual passion fueled his need for her.

"Brady," she murmured into his mouth.

The throaty sound of her voice abraded his nerve endings.

They were in a very private place. No one was likely to disturb them here. His free hand slipped under her shirt, stroking across the silky skin of her back. He was on the verge of doing something very foolish and he was helpless to stop it. Until he moved to brace his back and bumped against the shelves, sending a pile of scrub suits raining down on them.

Her startled exclamation made his eyes snap open. When he remembered where they were—and why—he muttered a curse under his breath.

"Sorry."

"We're both…off balance," she said in a breathy voice.

"Yeah," he agreed. One minute he was wondering if he could trust her, and in the next, he was getting ready to make love to her—in a supply closet.

He wanted to ask her whom she'd been calling when she emerged from the ladies' room with her phone in her hand, but he understood that doing it now would be a defense mechanism.

She stepped away from him and began picking up the packages. He did the same, shoving them back onto the shelves. Then she unwrapped one and pulled a blue scrub suit on over her jeans and shirt. Hurriedly, Brady also donned medical garb, including a cap to go over his hair.

When both of them looked as if they were ready to step into the operating room, he gave her a closer inspection. With her face cleaned up and her hospital outfit, she didn't look much like the woman who had come in here, but he couldn't be sure the disguise would hold up under intense scrutiny.

Opening the door a crack, he saw that the coast was clear.

"We'd better not walk together."

"Okay."

"The main hospital entrance is probably our best bet for getting a cab. Wait a couple of minutes before following me."

She nodded, and he checked the hallway again. Still clear, and he stepped out the door, wondering if he was going to see her again. If she wanted to escape from him, this was a good chance. Or had she figured out that she was safer with him than anywhere else?

GRACE WATCHED BRADY leave, thinking that this might be a good time to disappear—and make sure he could never find her again. But then what? She was still in bad trouble. Someone had killed Karen a little while ago—and tried to take Grace and Brady with her. She had no doubt they would try again.

Was she safer with her new bodyguard than without him? And what about that kiss? She was still tingling from the aftereffects and still wondering why she hadn't pushed him away.

She should have done that. She was getting in-volved with Brady Lockwood on too many different levels. It could be that her attraction to him was a good reason for running.

Of course, that might be backward reasoning.

She pressed her fist against her mouth. She'd been lying about a lot of things since he'd saved her from the goons in the alley. If she stayed with him, he was going to keep questioning her. And eventually she'd have to tell him the truth about herself. Was she prepared to do that?

More to the point, was she prepared for his reaction?

Glancing at the clock, she saw that two minutes had ticked by. Not entirely sure what she was going to do, she pulled open the door and saw a man striding rapidly down the hall, looking into rooms. She didn't need a positive ID to know this was the shooter from the house. He was searching for them—so he could finish what he'd started.

After easing the door closed, she turned toward the shelves, grabbed an armful of the scrub-suit packages and pretended that she was replacing the stock. The whole room smelled like smoke. Was that going to give her away? Scanning the shelves, she found a bottle of alcohol, unscrewed the top and sprinkled the pungent liquid around the supply closet, praying that would mask the fire odor.

When the door opened, she tried not to stiffen her body as she kept working.

## Chapter Nine

Grace could feel the man's gaze boring into her, but apparently he didn't recognize her from the back in this outfit.

After a moment, the door closed, and she let out the breath she'd been holding.

She wanted to flee the little room, but she forced herself to stay where she was. The guy had already checked here. He wouldn't come back, would he?

BRADY SPOTTED a sign pointing toward the front lobby, then kept his head down as he walked rapidly along the corridor.

He hated leaving Grace back there. For a whole lot of reasons. Like, could he trust her to meet him?

He needed more information from her, which was a good reason to stay with her. That was an excellent rationalization. Although it was true, but he knew he had his own reasons for keeping her close.

Thinking it wasn't a good idea to wait in the open, he paused and scanned the area, then saw an administrative office a few yards from the lobby entrance. As though he had some business to conduct, he stepped inside and held the door open a crack, looking out.

"Can I help you?" the woman behind the desk asked.

He pivoted to face her. "I told my wife I'd meet her here."

Her brow wrinkled. "This is isn't a public area."

"I realize that. I'm sorry. But we're new here, and she doesn't know the hospital well." Embroidering the story, he added, "She wants me to look at a house the real-estate agent showed her."

He turned again and looked out the door. To his relief, he saw Grace walking rapidly along the hallway, her gaze fixed on the lobby.

"Found her," he said to the woman at the desk as he stepped out of the office and started toward the main entrance, assuming that Grace would follow.

He had just reached the door when the man he'd spotted earlier stepped into view. The guy gave the lobby a quick look, then turned to scan the covered entranceway outside.

While his back was turned, Brady came up behind him, shoving him hard. He made a groaning sound as his face slammed into the wall.

People had turned to stare at them, and he spotted a security guard approaching.

"Go," he shouted to Grace.

She gave him a shocked look, then sprinted toward the door, past a woman being pushed along in a wheelchair.

A cab was waiting for the patient, and Brady made sure he got there first. "Sorry. My wife's ex is threatening to kill her," he shouted, pushing Grace into the back of the cab and climbing in behind her. "Go. Get out of here," he told the driver.

The cabbie looked confounded, but he pulled away from the curb. Brady leaned forward. "Drive away. Hurry. Before he starts shooting."

Looking through the back window, Brady saw that the thug had recovered and was standing on the curb, staring at the cab, his hand inside his jacket as if he was reaching for a gun. But he apparently decided not to risk a shot in the hospital driveway, not with the security guard bearing down on him.

Whirling, he charged toward the parking lot, and Brady prayed that he wasn't going to get his vehicle before they were out of sight.

The cab tore down the street, then rounded a corner. "Drive to the downtown area," Brady ordered. A few months ago, he'd been hired by a wife who was sure her husband was having an affair. He'd followed the guy around Frederick and found out that he was seeing someone else. Not another woman but a man. They'd met at several local restaurants, so Brady was familiar with the city.

"I don't want any trouble," the cabbie said.

"We'll get out as soon as I know we're not being followed." In the backseat, he started pulling off the medical garb.

Grace did the same.

"What the hell are you doing? Getting undressed?" the driver demanded.

"Just getting into civilian clothes."

"You smell like you've been in a chimney."

"We were in a big-time fire drill," Brady answered.

They headed for the restored area at the heart of the small city.

"Okay. This is what I'm looking for," Brady said when they'd driven a couple of blocks past shops and restaurants.

The driver pulled to the curb, and they both

got out, leaving the scrub suits in the backseat. Brady paid the fare, then took Grace's arm, ushering her toward a restaurant. When the cab was lost in traffic, he stopped short.

"Other way."

"Why?"

"He dropped us off here, and, if anybody asks, this is where he'll say we went."

Switching directions, he led her down the block and around the corner to a small hotel that the two men had used on some of their trysts.

As he walked toward the door, Grace asked, "What about the smoke?"

"We can't do much about it yet."

They both stepped into the small reception area, and Grace hung back, holding the door open.

A woman came bustling out from a room marked Office.

"Can I help you?"

Brady kept his voice even. "We'd like a room for the afternoon."

The woman looked him up and down, then eyed Grace. "I don't do less than twenty-four hours," she said.

Brady nodded.

"That will be a hundred and ten dollars."

He wanted to object.

Grace came forward and pulled out her wallet, then counted out the money.

The woman sniffed as she pushed the register book toward them. He wrote "Mr. and Mrs. James Stewart," gave 43 Light Street in Baltimore as the address, then took the key to room 207.

"Second floor, turn to the right," the woman said.

She kept her eyes on them as they climbed the stairs.

"She made me feel like a criminal," Grace said when they'd closed the door to the room behind them.

It was furnished with a relentless antiques theme, with tiny prints, wicker furniture and a clunky old television on the antique bureau.

As he looked back at Grace, he saw she was shaking. She'd been through a lot in the past few hours. She more than he.

The vulnerable look in her eyes made his insides clench. He reached for her, wrapping her in his arms, holding on to her. He'd started something earlier in the supply closet. Something he couldn't finish there. But now they were alone in a bedroom, and he pictured himself lowering his hand to her bottom, so he could press her more firmly against himself. Somehow he hung on to enough sanity to keep his hands above her waist.

She didn't have to stay in his arms. She could have pulled away, but she didn't move, didn't stir. Instead, she raised her face to his, putting her mouth a few tempting inches from his. The invitation was too much to resist. With a sound deep in his throat, he lowered his head so that his mouth brushed against hers.

The light contact wasn't enough for either of them. Within seconds they were tasting, sipping, nibbling.

Unable to keep his hands still, he let them rove restlessly over her back, her shoulders. The more he touched her, the more frantic he became to take in as much of her as he could.

The bed was only a few feet away. They could be off their feet in seconds. He tried to tell himself he didn't know her well enough for that—until her hands began to stroke over his back and shoulders in a restless rhythm while the kiss turned more frantic.

Conscious thought left him as blood pounded through his veins and pooled in the lower part of his body.

He had been alone for a long time because that was the way he'd wanted it, and it hadn't been all that difficult. He'd simply made sure that he wasn't in a position to get close to anybody. Until he met Grace.

As he kissed her, he silently acknowledged that he needed more, so much more, from her.

More than she was willing to give?

No. She was warm and pliant in his arms, as

caught up in the emotions of the moment as he was himself.

Through two layers of fabric, he could feel the points of her nipples abrading his chest.

Erotic images assaulted him. His fingers ached with the need to stroke back and forth against those tight points. Or better yet, pulling up her blouse and lowering his head so that he could suck her into his mouth, and circle one of the tempting nubs with his tongue.

Somehow he kept from going that far, but he couldn't stop himself from bringing his hands inward to press against the side of her breasts.

The world had contracted to a small space— with room for only himself and the woman in his arms. Yet some impulse toward sanity made him lift his head. Or maybe it was mistrust. He still didn't know how Grace fit into his brother's murder, and he was going to find out before he got any more involved with her.

"We can't," he managed to say in a strangled voice.

Her eyes blinked open, and she stared at

him—confused and then wounded looking. Yet he saw resignation, too.

When she took a step back, he dragged in a breath and let it out.

Perhaps because she didn't know what else to do, she picked up the TV remote, flipped on the set and started running through the channels.

"Stop."

She lifted her finger from the button, and they both stared at a news feature on John Ridgeway—the man whose death had started this whole crazy episode.

He stared transfixed at the screen, seeing shots of a younger John Ridgeway—shots that looked a hell of a lot like Kevin Parsons, the young man John had asked Brady to locate.

Yeah, Parsons must be his illegitimate son, all right. Only now John was never going to get a chance to meet him. Brady thought about his own less-than-ideal childhood. He knew Parsons had been raised by loving adoptive parents who had sent him to an Ivy League college. Probably if he told the kid about his real father, that would only add a disruptive element to his life. Better to leave well enough alone.

Another thought struck him, and he pulled his cell phone out of his pocket. Lydia was probably watching this program, too. Over and over, the way they repeated news items on the cable channels. Probably he could risk a short call to her.

"I should call my sister-in-law," he said to Grace.

She nodded. "I'll be washing off the smoke smell."

She stepped into the bathroom, and he heard the shower running. When he clicked on the phone, he found a dozen messages from Lydia. She answered his return call immediately.

"Brady, where are you?"

"I ran into some problems."

"Why aren't you here?"

He wasn't going to tell her that men were

trying to kill him—and it all went back to John's death.

"I would be if I could," he answered.

He heard her voice rise. "You're John's brother. He left you a lot of money. The least you can do is show up for his funeral."

"He did?" Brady asked in surprise.

"A lot more than you deserve." She laughed. "You're a millionaire."

"I don't want his money."

"Too bad. If you weren't so focused on your own pitiful life, you might be able to enjoy it." She switched back to her own agenda. "Everyone's going to wonder where you are."

Right. Appearances were important to Lydia.

"I'm sorry."

"I'm tired of making excuses for you."

"What's that supposed to mean?" he answered, struggling to keep his voice even.

"Are you holed up somewhere drinking?"

"No! I'm trying to find out what happened to John."

"You found that woman—his mistress?"

He glanced toward the bathroom door. "If you mean Grace Cunningham, I found her, but she's not his mistress."

Lydia scoffed. "She spun you a story and you fell for it."

"No. We're investigating John's death."

"We? She's with you?"

"I can't talk about this over the phone."

"Then come give me the support I need." He could tell now that her voice was slightly slurred. If anyone had been drinking, it was Lydia.

He sighed. "The investigation has put me in danger. If I come to your house, it will put you in danger, too."

She gave a nasty laugh. "That's a pretty pitiful excuse for doing exactly what you want to."

"It's the truth. Lydia, I'm sorry. I'll be there as soon as I can."

"In time for the funeral?"

"I hope so."

"Well, if you can't get here to bury your brother, don't come at all."

He'd planned to make the call short. Instead he found himself apologizing to his sister-in-law and trying to make her understand that he'd be there if he could.

Finally, he hung up, knowing that she was still mad as hell. And there was nothing he could do about it.

When he'd clicked off the phone and looked up, Grace was watching him. She'd taken a quick shower and washed and dried her hair. And she'd freshened up her clothing.

"I take it that call didn't go well."

"No," he muttered, unwilling to go over it all over again.

"What are we going to do?"

He looked down at his Rolex. "I can pawn my watch and get some cash."

"I brought cash."

"We need a laptop computer—and a car. And some fresh clothing." He kept his gaze fixed on her. "And we need to have a serious talk."

Her expression turned resigned. "I know."

"What aren't you telling me?"

She swallowed. "It's complicated."

"You'll feel better if you just come clean with me."

"I doubt it."

"I'll give you some time to think about it." He stepped into the bathroom, thinking he should press her, yet hoping she'd start talking on her own. To give her some space, he took a quick shower, then shook out his shirt and pants and climbed back into them.

When he stepped back into the bedroom, Grace was staring at the television.

"Ready to talk."

"Yes."

"What were you to my brother?"

"His research assistant, like I told you."

"What were you to Karen Hilliard?"

She hesitated before she spoke. "She had some information for me that I couldn't ignore."

Before she could say anything more, a knock sounded at the door.

Like in his apartment. Only this was different.

He glanced at the door, then at the window and froze. Two men were standing on the porch roof right outside—pointing guns at them.

## Chapter Ten

Grace watched in horror as one of the men raised his hand and smashed the butt of his gun against the windowpane, which shattered under the impact. At the same time, the door burst inward and another gunman filled the doorway. She'd seen one of the men before, at the hospital, but now he had reinforcements.

Brady moved to her left, his arm sliding around her waist and pulling her protectively against his side, but he said nothing.

The guy in the doorway gave Brady a smirking look. "I guess you should have gotten off the phone a little faster."

Brady answered with a curse.

"We're getting out of here. If you give us any trouble, your girlfriend gets it first. Got that?"

Grace cringed.

"She's not my girlfriend."

"You look pretty cozy. You want me to shoot her now?"

She gasped. "Don't."

"Then let's go."

"Where?" Brady demanded.

"Where we can have a nice chat."

A chat? Was that what they wanted? Or were they going someplace private where these guys could do anything?

One of the men on the roof reached through the ruined window and turned the locking mechanism. Then he pushed up the sash and stepped inside.

Grace could feel Brady tensing beside her, and she hoped he wasn't going to try anything heroic because the odds were not in their favor at the moment.

"In case you're hoping for some help, the

lady who owns this place is out. So we're all going to walk downstairs, then out the front door and get into the car that's pulled up at the curb. Got it?"

"Yes," Brady answered in a low voice. His lips were set in a grim line, and she knew he was angry with himself for calling his sister-in-law.

One man walked in front of them. The two from the porch walked behind. They all proceeded down the steps, then out into the late-afternoon sunshine.

Grace kept hoping that someone on the street would see what was happening and call the police. But there was nobody to witness the strained procession.

Two cars waited at the curb. When the men ushered her toward one and Brady toward the other, she felt panic rise in her throat. It wasn't until that moment that she realized how much she'd come to depend on him. She was sure his bodyguard offer had started off as a ploy. But he had a way of making her feel safe, even when she knew it was only an illusion. Unfortunately, there was nothing he could do for her now.

The thug pushed her into the backseat and followed her inside, keeping her covered with the gun.

One of the men in front pulled out a cell phone and began to talk in a low voice.

"We've got them…. Yeah. Okay."

Who was he taking to? She strained to hear the other side of the conversation, but it was muffled.

Her focus was on the man talking, and before she realized what was happening, the guy beside her pressed a cloth over her nose and mouth. She tried to fight him off, but the vapors coming from the cloth robbed her of strength. Then the world went black.

SHE DIDN'T KNOW how much time passed. Sometime later, she swam back to consciousness.

"Grace?"

"Um?"

When she opened her eyes, she was lying on a narrow bed, and Brady was sitting beside her, chafing her hand. "Finally."

"How long was I out?"

"A few hours."

"Oh Lord," she answered, fighting to put strength into her voice. "They didn't do it to you?"

"No. Are you all right?"

She took a mental inventory, flexed her arms and legs. Her head still felt a little fuzzy, but she answered, "Yes. Are you?"

"Yes."

When she tried to sit up, her head spun and she flopped back against the thin pillow.

"You're not okay," he muttered, stroking his fingers against her cheek.

"I'm just a little dizzy." From where she lay on the narrow bed, she looked around. They were in a small bedroom, about ten feet by ten feet. The walls were rough wood, and she got the feeling they were in a vacation cabin. "Where are we?"

"I don't know. They put a hood over my head. But I'd guess we're a couple of hours from Frederick. In the mountains. Maybe a vacation cabin."

"Why didn't they put you out, too?"

"I don't know."

"Can we get away?"

"I don't know," he answered again.

He squeezed her hand, then climbed off the bed and walked to the small window. Following him with her eyes, she saw that there were bars on the outside of the glass. Could they break the glass and remove the bars? Probably not.

Beyond the window, she saw what appeared to be a forest.

As she switched her gaze back to the room, she saw that there was no furniture—apart from the one bed, which was bolted to the floor. To the side of the bed was a metal bucket, which she assumed was going to be their toilet.

While she tried to come up with a plan, a noise at the door made her head jerk in that direction. Pushing herself up, she let her feet drop to the floor as two of the thugs stepped inside the room. Both of them were holding guns. Four men had picked up her and Brady at the hotel. Were the others gone?

Both of the men gave her a long look, then focused on Brady. "Start talking," the closer one said.

"About what?" Brady shot back.

"Time to tell us what you know."

"You mean that Grace was in the next room when my brother died—and now you're after the two of us."

The man made a scoffing sound. "You can do better than that."

"Believe me, that's about it."

"Oh, come on."

Brady shrugged. "If you're planning to use enhanced interrogation techniques, forget it. I don't know anything. But it's been proven that a guy being tortured will say anything to get the pain to stop. So you won't know if I'm telling the truth or not."

The man was silent for a long moment. "I think you know more than you're saying," he said. "And I think you've gotten close to Ms. Cunningham. Or maybe you already knew her before Ridgeway died."

She saw Brady's jaw clench.

Ignoring him, the man kept talking. "I'm going to bet that the most effective way to get the information out of you is to use some of those 'creative techniques' on Ms. Cunningham. Well—you'll be involved, too. We'll tie you up and give you a ringside seat while we rape her. Do you think that would get you to talk?"

Grace gasped as terrible images leaped into her head. They'd found Karen handcuffed to a bed with her panties off and her skirt around her waist. Had these men done that to her? She cringed away from them.

Brady stepped in front of her. "Stay away from her."

The guy made a scoffing sound. "You're in no position to make demands. But we'll give you a little time to think about it." The two men backed out of the room, leaving her and Brady alone.

Unable to stop herself from shaking, she turned pleading eyes toward him.

Lifting her off the bed, he wrapped his arms around her and held her close.

She leaned into him, comforted by his strength. "Would they do that?" she asked in a voice that she couldn't hold steady.

"I don't know, but I don't want to find out."

"What are we going to do?"

"Get out of here," he growled as he held her and stroked her.

Closing her eyes, she rested her head on his shoulder. "I'm sorry. I got you into a mess," she whispered.

He tensed, and she could feel him making an effort to relax. "We'll talk about it later." As he spoke, he looked pointedly around the room, and she realized that there could be a microphone picking up their conversation. Maybe that was part of the men's plan. She didn't know who they were. Not for sure. But she could make an educated guess.

Outside the room, she could hear the sound of muffled voices. Brady eased away and put his finger to his lips. Then he crossed the room, and she followed, watching him press his ear against the door as he tried to find out what the men were saying.

Moving beside him, she did the same, but she couldn't hear any distinct words. But moments later, a car engine started.

Brady stepped away from the door and put his mouth to her ear. In a barely audible whisper, he said, "At least one of them left, which gives us better odds. You lie down and start calling out for help. Tell them that stuff they gave you made you sick."

She nodded, crossed back to the bed and lay down, watching as Brady flattened himself against the wall on the side where the open door would hide him.

When he was in position, she took a deep breath, screwed up her face and started crying out.

"Help me. You've got to help me. Please, somebody help me. I'm so sick."

From the other side of the door, a voice shouted, "What the hell is going on in there?"

"Help me. That stuff you gave me made me feel like I'm going to die. Help me."

"It'll wear off."

"No," she gasped out.

Long seconds passed, and nothing happened. Her gaze shot to Brady, then away.

"Call him again," he mouthed.

"Please. Don't leave me like this. I think I'm dying."

When the doorknob turned, Brady tensed, waiting to find out if they had a chance.

As one of the men stepped cautiously into the room, gun in hand, Brady sprang forward, coming down on the man's back, pushing him toward the floor.

The man grunted and tried to twist around

to get his weapon into position to fire, but Grace snatched up the metal bucket beside the bed and crashed it down on his head. He went limp.

Brady rolled the man over, smashed a fist into his chin and took the gun from his hand. Then he whirled toward the door, ready for reinforcements. But the doorway was empty. Brady stepped out of their makeshift cell. Grace followed. Like their prison, the room was roughly made but furnished with several comfortable easy chairs and a couch. Along one wall was a kitchen unit.

Brady turned and closed the cell door, locking the thug inside.

"We'd better get out of here."

She followed him across the wood floor, where he stood listening at the door, then cautiously opened it, not knowing what they'd find.

When Brady stepped outside and looked back, he saw a small log cabin with a sagging roof. A gravel road led down a steep incline away from the building. Parked a few yards away was one of the cars they'd come in.

"Transportation." He crossed to the driver's door, and checked inside and found the keys.

"Get in."

As they started down the hill, Grace let out the breath she must have been holding.

"Is this the only road out of here?" she whispered.

"Looks like it. So we'd better make tracks."

Soon they were hurtling down the narrow gravel road.

Beside him, Grace was holding tight to the handle above the passenger door. "Slow down. We're not going to get away if we crash."

"Yeah." He moved his foot to the brake and pressed. When nothing happened, he pumped the pedal. Still nothing.

"Shit!"

"What's wrong?"

"No brakes," he shouted while the car continued to pick up speed as it flew down the narrow mountain track.

"But they just used this car."

"Maybe."

He pulled up on the parking brake—to no effect. He'd thought he'd released it. Now he wondered if it had really been engaged. Gripping the wheel, he struggled to keep the vehicle on the narrow road, his mind racing for some way out of this mess. He'd thought he was so clever, breaking them out of their prison, but it looked as if it had been a trap. He'd thought their guards had been careless, but the bastards had been careless on purpose, setting him and Grace up to die in their escape attempt.

Their bodies would be found in a mangled car. Brady Lockwood—with his brother's supposed mistress. Then conspiracy theory would take over. If anyone was going to get blamed for John's death, it was them.

This was the second attempt, he realized. If they'd been blown up with Karen, the same conspiracy scenario would have played out.

Ahead of him, the trees opened up, and he

saw to his horror that there was a steep drop-off on the left and no guardrail. On the right were trees and boulders.

The car kept picking up speed as it approached the cliff edge, and he could think of only one way to get them out of this alive.

"Hang on, I'm going to try and slow us down."

Grace sucked in a sharp breath as he eased toward the forest, looking for a break in the trees.

"What are you doing?"

"Hold tight."

She grasped the edges of her seat with white-knuckled hands as he eased off the road and into the woods. Metal screeched as the fender hit a boulder, then tore off. The car kept going, moving farther off the road, the dirt and leaves under the tires helping to slow them. But not enough. When he saw a break in the trees, he plunged in, scraping the sides of the car against massive trunks, turning the wheel sharply, trying to slow them without scoring a direct hit against anything.

He was perilously close to disaster as he wove through the trees, increasing the drag on the car and praying that the sides weren't going to cave in.

"It's leveling off ahead," Grace called out.

"Yeah. And muddy."

Changing his strategy, he drove into the mire, feeling the tires sink into the goop. The boggy surface slowed their forward progress considerably.

"Hang on," he advised, as he gripped the wheel and headed for a pine tree, thumping against the trunk and coming to a rocking halt.

"Out of the car," he ordered. "They could be waiting for us around the next curve."

When Grace tried to comply, she found the passenger door was so battered that it wouldn't open.

"Come out this way."

He slid out, then helped her across the seat.

When he tugged her out of the car, she fell into his arms. For a long moment, they clung together, each of them shaking as they absorbed the impact of the near miss.

"You're a hell of a driver, Brady."

"Thanks to my reckless youth. And luck." He lifted his head and looked around. "We can't stay here."

"I know. But I'm not sure my knees will hold me up."

"Just put one foot in front of the other." Taking her hand, he led her rapidly into the woods.

They headed away from the road, and he stopped when he saw moving lights in the distance.

"Where are we?" she asked.

"Could be Maryland, Virginia or West Virginia," he answered. "They're all close enough to Frederick."

"Those men. They wanted us to get into the car."

"Yeah. Victims of an unfortunate accident."

She winced as they kept moving toward the lights, which seemed to be the headlights of moving vehicles.

Breaking through the woods, they found themselves on a rural road, this one two lanes and paved.

"How long before the bad guys find out we're not dead?" Grace asked.

"Depends on how long they planned to stay away. But they could come back along this route."

When more headlight beams cut through the gathering darkness, he led her behind a large, crumbling building that might once have been a barn.

After the car passed, they kept walking until they came to a crossroad. A gas station sat on one of the corners, and the lot in back of it was filled with cars—many of which had seen better days.

"Wait here."

Brady looked around to make sure they weren't being observed, then selected a twenty-year-old Chevy and opened the door. It smelled like cigarette smoke, and the floor was littered with a collection of fast-food wrappers and bags. Easing down behind the dash, he found the wires that would start the engine. With a silent prayer, he twisted them together, and the motor caught.

The gas gauge was a quarter full.

"Come on," he called softly.

Grace climbed into the passenger seat. "We're stealing this car?"

He shrugged. "You do what you have to. My brother taught me that."

She still looked upset, so he added, "It's not worth much. I'm hoping nobody misses it for a while."

He pulled onto the road and headed for a destination unknown, with Grace sitting tense and silent beside him.

He wanted to ask if she had any idea who the men were who had tried to kill them. But he kept silent because he was going to be looking into her eyes when he asked her any more questions. He wasn't fooling himself. He'd wanted to protect her when he thought she was in danger, but he was sure she knew more than she was saying.

When they came to a road sign, he found out they were twenty miles from Martinsburg, West Virginia. Outside of town, he pulled into the parking lot of a discount department store.

"What are you doing?"

"We're still wearing the clothes from the fire. We need to change. Luckily, the thugs didn't take our money. But I guess they wanted our personal effects on us, so we could be easily identified."

"You think of everything," she murmured.

"I'm trying. Stay here."

She nodded and scrunched down in her seat. In record time, he bought them both jeans and T-shirts and toiletries. He was back in less than fifteen minutes.

At a highway gas station, he told her to change her clothes in the ladies' room. When she returned, he ducked into the men's room and changed, then drove on into the night.

His next stop was a fast-food drive-through where they got burgers and milk shakes— since he figured they needed the calories. He ate while he drove, putting fifty miles on the odometer before he decided it was safe to stop.

Knowing that many of the houses in the area were vacation homes, he picked a driveway and turned in. When he got halfway to the house and saw lights on, he backed up and drove a few hundred feet down the road. On the third try, he found a house that was dark, and he parked around back.

"Wait here while I make sure it's empty."

"I'm coming with you."

He gave her an exasperated look. He wanted to order her to stay in the car until he'd made sure they were alone here. But he knew it would only make her more adamant.

She followed him across the back deck to the

door. It took only a few moments to find the key hidden under a flowerpot.

Once they were inside, he put the safety chain in the door and turned on a lamp. They were in a nicely furnished living room, with country touches like throws and wicker baskets. He made a quick trip through the house, making sure they were alone. When he returned to the living room, Grace was still in the same position by the door.

She looked at him. "I didn't thank you for saving me."

"We're not in the clear yet."

She nodded. "What are we going to do?"

"That partly depends on you," he answered.

"Me?"

"On whether you start telling me the truth."

A kind of desperate look came into her eyes. Before he could put some distance between them, she reached for him and wrapped her arms around him, pressing her face against his chest.

"Don't."

"I want to be close to you," she said in a low voice. "Don't push me away."

## Chapter Eleven

Disentangling himself would be the smart thing to do. But at the moment, Brady didn't have the strength to be smart. Well, maybe he was making progress. Not so long ago, after a death ride down the side of a mountain, he would have gone straight to a liquor store. Now all he wanted was to hold on to Grace Cunningham.

Whatever else he might have said to her turned into a long sigh of pleasure as she worked her hands under his T-shirt and pressed them flat against his back before she started stroking his skin in a slow, sensual pattern.

He'd told himself he was through with relationships, but Grace had worked her way past the barrier he'd erected. So far, he'd pulled back every time things got too heavy. Until now.

Too much had happened too quickly for him to guard his emotions. He needed to give into the pleasure of holding her, touching her, kissing her.

When she lifted her face to him, their mouths met in a kiss that was fueled by sexual need and by the terror of their captivity.

He turned his head first one way and then the other, his mouth moving over hers, allowing himself to feast on her.

As he took a step back, she made a small sound of protest—until she saw that he was pulling his shirt over his head and tossing it onto the chair.

Her gaze on him, she pulled off her T-shirt, then reached to unfasten her bra.

He saw the sudden flash of nerves in her eyes

and knew that despite her show of boldness, she didn't make a habit of seduction.

"You're sure about this?" he made himself ask.

"Very sure."

When she moved into his arms, he groaned at the soft pressure of her breasts against his chest, his arousal ratcheting up to a whole new level. They swayed together, touching, kissing, sighing.

Before his legs stopped working, he led her down a short hall to a bedroom, where he turned back the spread and the blanket, then caught her in his arms again, stroking her back and shoulders while she reached between them.

When her hands came to rest on his belt buckle, he went very still. His arms at his sides, he watched her as she unbuckled the belt, then started on his jeans.

His breath caught as she lowered his zipper and slid her hand into the opening she'd made, working her way beneath the elastic band of

his briefs to cup his aching erection. For wonderful seconds, he let himself enjoy the pleasure of her touch before he forced himself to
stop her.

"Enough."

He lifted her hand away from his taut flesh
before unzipping her jeans and easing them
down her legs.

They both kicked their pants away.

Taking her down to the surface of the bed, he
gathered her to him, hoping he could contain
his urgency.

When his hands found her breasts, her long
sigh of pleasure told him how much she liked
him teasing her nipples between his finger-
tips. He followed the caress of his fingers with
his lips, hardly able to believe that anything
could feel so good in his mouth as her aroused
flesh.

One of her hands cupped the back of his
head, holding her to him, while the other
stroked restlessly over his back and shoulders.

He marveled at the tender, possessive feelings that welled up inside him.

He shifted his mouth to her neck, then her jaw, then finally her lips, kissing her as he slid his hand into the soft folds of her most intimate flesh.

She was swollen and wet for him, her hips moving restlessly as he brought her up to the level where he wanted her.

She clutched his shoulders, her fingers digging into his tense muscles. But he stayed where he was, entranced by the feel of her and by the sounds of pleasure she was making for him.

"Brady, you're going to tip me over the edge."

The urgency in her voice made it impossible to wait.

Taking her mouth in a long, passionate kiss, he moved over her. She reached between them, guiding the hard shaft of his erection to herself, and he drove forward, his body merging with hers.

For a moment both of them went very still. Then he began to move within her, slowly at first, then quickening the pace when he could no longer hold back.

As his hand slipped between them to stroke her, he felt her inner muscles contract around him, and when she came undone for him, he felt the shattering explosion of pleasure take him.

GRACE LAY ON the bed, turning her head so she could look at Brady. When she'd accepted him as her bodyguard, she'd had no idea of how strong and competent—how extraordinary— he was. She'd told him she knew a lot about him from his brother. That was only part of the truth. She'd read up on him on her own, studied him. She had felt as if she was getting to know him long before they ever met.

Back then, she hadn't understood the totality of the man. Now she knew that, if she'd been hiring a bodyguard, she couldn't have picked a better one. But it was more than that.

She'd developed strong feelings for him. She'd wanted to make love with him for her own selfish reasons. She'd wanted that—even if he ended up hating her later.

Easing out of bed, she tiptoed across to the closet, where she found a man's shirt she could wear. After slipping into it, she gave Brady a long look. He seemed to be sleeping, but had she seen his eyelids flicker?

She stood very still, waiting. When he didn't move, she rolled up the sleeves of the shirt and walked into the adjoining bathroom, where she quietly closed the door and clicked on the light. When her eyes had adjusted to the brightness, she turned toward the mirror.

Back at the house in Frederick, Karen had been clawing at her arm and had ripped a hole in the fabric of her blouse. Below it, Grace had seen a bluish mark that had startled her. Because she'd seen it on herself.

Pulling her right arm out of the shirt-sleeve, she raised her arm and looked at the bluish place that she'd always thought was a birthmark. But it was just like the mark she'd seen on Karen. A brand!

White-faced, she was staring at herself in the mirror, when the bathroom door burst open, and Brady plowed inside. He'd pulled his jeans back on but hadn't bothered with a shirt.

The thought struck her that between the two of them, they had a full set of clothing. Not exactly dressed if the homeowners showed up.

"What are you doing?" he demanded.

Their eyes met in the mirror. "I...I was trying not to wake you up."

"Yeah, I can see that. You're up to something."

"What makes you think so?"

"Most people make some kind of noise in a bathroom. Like from the sink, the shower or the toilet."

"How observant of you," she muttered.

"Yeah. My detective skills."

She wanted to slip her arm back into the sleeve, but Brady had already crossed the room and pulled the shirt aside. Turning her arm over, he stared at the blue circle.

"That's the same mark that was on Karen," he said in a gritty voice.

Unable to speak, she simply nodded.

"What—the two of you belong to a secret society?"

"Something like that."

"And you were sent to spy on me."

"No."

"This charade is over," he said in a voice that could have cut through ice.

Turning he walked back into the bedroom and grabbed his shirt.

"What are you doing?"

"I'm leaving—before you can contact your friends again—like you did while we were in the hospital." He gave her a hard look. "Was that whole thing at the bad guys' hideout a setup? They threatened to torture you—so I'd try to break out. Only they double-crossed you and put you in the death car with me?"

"No. They didn't put me anywhere. I got in myself."

Ignoring that, he asked another question. "And why did you seduce me a little while ago? Was that part of the plan?"

"I didn't seduce you. We made love."

"You can call it that." He sighed. "Too bad I can't believe a thing you say. I think if I'm going to stay alive, I'm better off on my own."

When he started toward the front door, she ran after him and grabbed his arm. "Wait."

Without turning back to her, he asked, "Why should I?"

"Because I'll tell you everything," she said in a whisper, dreading what was to come.

His voice was still hard as forged steel. "This could be interesting. One way or the other."

"What does that mean?"

"I'll have to figure out if you're telling me the truth or a fairy story."

He turned on the overhead light in the dining room and gestured toward one of the pressed-back oak chairs.

"Sit down."

She sat and buttoned the long shirt that was still gaping open.

Brady pulled out the chair on the other side of the table and sat down, facing her.

"Let's start with something easy. Whom did you call when we were at the hospital?"

Easy? The question made her want to leap up and run, but she stayed where she was. "Kevin Parsons," she answered in a small voice.

"Kevin Parsons. You expect me to believe that?"

"I hope so. It's the truth."

"You got that name from…from my brother's files."

"No. Kevin and I have been in contact for a couple of years. I was calling to tell him what happened in Frederick," she answered, fighting to keep her voice steady.

He made a scoffing sound. "I don't know why I'm still sitting here. Okay let's try another one—were you part of a conspiracy to kill my brother?"

She felt the blood drain from her face. "I was Karen's lookout," she managed to say.

Brady looked as if he wanted to lunge out of his chair, but he stayed where he was. "And you've been playing me for a fool since I found you outside your apartment."

"No. Let me tell you the rest of it," she begged, her hands clenched in her lap. The irony of the situation tore at her. She'd fought as hard as she could to keep her secrets. Now she was begging Brady to listen to the truth.

His eyes glittered with menace as he stared at her. "You helped kill my brother."

"Because he was going to kill Kevin."

He flung a curse at her. "That makes no sense. Kevin is his son. He asked me to locate him."

She shook her head. "I'm sorry. Your brother was using you, the way he used so many people. Ridgeway didn't ask you to locate his illegitimate son. Kevin isn't his child. He's his clone."

"What?"

"His clone. Your brother's heart was damaged when he was exposed to chemical agents in Vietnam. He was getting worse, and he was going to solve the problem by using Kevin as an organ donor."

Brady kept his gaze fixed on her, and she wanted to squirm away, but she forced herself to sit calmly, facing him.

"You really expect me to believe a story as wild as that?"

"What? You don't think your brother is ruthless enough to sacrifice another person's life?"

She could tell she'd gotten to him with that question. Still, she kept her hands clenched in her lap as she continued with her explanation.

"Thirty years ago, Dr. Richard Cortez perfected a human-cloning process. He kept his research quiet, but you might have heard of him when his lab in Bethesda blew up six months ago. He was killed."

Brady nodded. "I read about it."

"Cortez needed initial funding for his

research, and rich men and women were offered the opportunity to have a clone made of themselves. You could join a program that would provide you with spare parts. Only there's a gatekeeper who decides when someone is sick enough to require a transplant. He's also the man who knows where to find the clones."

"Who is he?"

"He calls himself the Paladin. I don't know who he is. But he denied your brother's request."

"Why?"

"I assume because he didn't think the situation was critical enough, but Ridgeway wanted the heart transplant, so he had you go looking for Kevin."

"Kevin was adopted!"

"That's right. In addition to the production laboratory, there was an adoption program. All of the clones were adopted by couples desperate to have children. The couples bore the expense of raising the children. A very neat arrangement."

Brady rocked back in his seat. "Why should I believe any of this? What proof do you have?"

"Cortez liked to play God—to find out how far he could go with his research. Karen Hilliard was the one who discovered the clone plot. She and Kevin were both Ridgeway's clones."

"How can that be?"

"Cortez genetically turned off genes on Karen's Y chromosome so she wouldn't have male sexual characteristics. Karen was physically a woman with a male chromosome. She found out when she failed to get her period in her teens. Like your brother, she was smart and inquisitive. After learning of her chromosome abnormality, she went digging into her background and discovered Cortez's clinic—and the adoption ring. And she wasn't willing to leave it at that.

"After breaking into the clinic's records, she

started contacting some of the other clones, including her 'twin brother,' Kevin. She was a natural leader, but you know that, too, because you know your brother. He built up a team of loyal men who worked for him at the Ridgeway Consortium."

As she finished the long speech, Grace studied the man sitting across the table from her. He sat silently, and she figured she was finally getting through to him. At least he was no longer angry.

But his next words showed her that he was still questioning her whole story. "Then why didn't Karen look like John?" he asked in a flat voice.

"Because she had plastic surgery to alter her appearance enough so that she wouldn't reveal herself. But she was still John's clone. That's why it was easy for her to seduce him. She understood him perfectly."

The sick look on Brady's face increased. "You're saying she made love with…herself."

Grace shrugged. "Like your brother, she was willing to do what was necessary."

"Let's assume all that's true. Where do you fit into the picture?"

She wanted to lower her head into her hands, but she forced herself to keep her gaze level. Instead she began unbuttoning her shirt. Pulling her right arm from the sleeve, she held it up, pointing to the mark on the underside of her arm. "I didn't know what this thing meant until I saw the same mark on Karen. Then I realized it must be the brand Cortez put on us."

She drew in a deep breath and told the secret she'd kept hidden all her life. "I'm a clone, too."

Brady could hardly speak. The words he was hearing were too much to comprehend. He could only stare at her.

His mind reeled. Before he could scratch the surface of his questions, Grace continued to explain. It was as if she wanted to tell him everything before she could rethink the wisdom of it.

"Karen had it," she told him as she pointed at the blue mark on her upper arm. "I'm sure you'll find it on Kevin, too. It probably has a serial number identifying us. After she recruited Kevin, Karen came to me, and explained about Cortez's project. And the gatekeeper guy—the Paladin. The plan to use us as needed."

He saw a look flash in her eyes but he couldn't identify it. He couldn't even think straight.

"She left out the part about the marks. Maybe she hadn't figured that out yet. Lucky for her she only had sex with John when they were in the office. If she'd gotten undressed, he would have seen it, although maybe he wouldn't have known what it was." She shrugged and looked away for a second. "But we made a pact. We vowed to fight back. The man who killed Cortez was one of us. He was a master bomber, but something must have gone wrong."

HE WAS FORCED into a corner. But he was going to get out of it, the Paladin thought, as he strode to the computer screen and called up a password-protected program. He'd ordered Brady and Grace Cunningham eliminated, and he'd thought his men had worked out a fool-proof plan to do it—which would make it look as if they'd killed themselves trying to escape after assassinating John Ridgeway.

That would have proved the conspiracy theory of Ridgeway's death—along with the information that was now planted at Brady Lockwood's apartment. The papers showed that Lockwood, Grace Cunningham and Karen Hilliard had plotted to kill Ridgeway so that Brady would inherit his share of the man's considerable estate.

Unfortunately, Lockwood and Cunningham had gotten away. Again. Which meant they were still dangerous.

And he had another problem.

He'd made up a fake conspiracy for public consumption. Now he was coming to the conclusion that he was dealing with a real one. As far as he could tell, the clones had started organizing against their masters. He'd hoped against hope that he was wrong, but there were simply too many deaths to ignore. And his best defense against the revolt was a good offense.

He had no way of knowing which of the clones were in on the rebellion. That meant that he was going to have to eliminate all of them.

On the computer screen, a list of names appeared. The list of the clones, with their serial numbers. But he could do better than that. Each of them had an identifier embedded under his or her skin. When they'd been young, there'd been no problem keeping track of them. But now he was going to use the advanced system.

Pressing a series of keys he sent a signal to the tags, and each of them began to emit a homing beacon, making it quick and easy to find the clones and have them killed.

Of course, a lot would get caught who weren't

part of the conspiracy, but they had always been expendable. Too bad the people who'd paid big bucks for a personal insurance policy were going to be angry when they found they couldn't cash it in. But better safe than sorry.

As he studied the computer screen, he saw that a lot of the conspirators were in the Maryland/Virginia/DC, area. Which was convenient because he had a team of men close by.

He began calling up random signals, checking the exact locations and stopped when he found that one of the transmitters was very close to the last known location of Brady Lockwood and Grace Cunningham.

A chill went up his spine. He'd been thinking that Grace Cunningham was only a loose end he had to tie up—a woman who had been at the wrong place at the wrong time. Now he wondered if she was one of the clones.

Going back to the list, he checked the names again. No Grace Cunningham. But if she was joining a conspiracy, she'd change her name. And probably her looks.

Reaching for the phone, he called the man who had let Cunningham and Lockwood get away.

BRADY SAT IN STUNNED silence. He hadn't wanted to believe a word Grace was saying. Obviously she was so desperate that she'd spun a fantastic story to convince him of something that couldn't possibly be true. But the more she'd talked, the more sense she made.

He'd always known his brother was smart and ruthless and willing to do what it took to get any task accomplished, no matter what the cost.

He also knew that John's heart had been damaged when he'd been exposed to chemical agents in Vietnam. In fact, he'd told Brady about it when he asked him to look for Kevin. He'd said that he wanted to do right by the boy, in case something happened to him.

Yeah, right by the boy.

He fought the sickness rising in his throat because too much of this fit into his knowledge of his brother.

"Do you believe me?" Grace finally asked him.

Brady's mouth was so dry that he had to swallow before he could speak. "Yes."

Grace's next words hit him like stones. "And now you're feeling dirty because you know you slept with a woman who's less than human."

# Chapter Twelve

"No!"

Brady scrambled out of his chair, rounded the table and pulled Grace up. Gathering her close, he wrapped his arms around her. "Never think that," he said, making each word count.

She began to speak again, her voice muffled as she pressed her face against his chest. "I lied to you when we first met. I kept lying. I knew who Karen was the whole time."

"I understand why you couldn't be straight with me."

She kept talking, giving him reasons not to trust her. "And I got you tangled up in some very dangerous business. You were right. There was a conspiracy to kill your brother, but only to save Kevin's life."

"Where is he?"

"I don't know exactly. But I can contact him. Well, for short periods of time. When I called him from the hospital, he made me get off pretty quickly."

"He was willing to stay out of the action?"

She made a small sound. "That's probably hard for you to believe, given your brother's personality. But he was willing to let Karen run this operation because he's also practical."

"Okay."

She pushed away. "Okay, what?"

He met her questioning gaze. "We'll find out who the Paladin is and stop him."

"You're saying you're going to switch your... mission?"

"Yes."

"Why?"

"I could give you a whole lot of answers. Like, my brother was using me."

"He dried you out after your wife died," she said, and he knew she was being ruthless in her efforts to put distance between them.

"Yeah. He did that—so I'd be grateful, and he could take advantage of my loyalty. But that's not the main reason I want to find the Paladin. The whole clone thing sickens me. It's got to be stopped."

"It's dangerous. I cut myself off completely from my family to make sure nothing happened to them."

"That's right. You told me you were adopted, too."

"Of course. But I had a very good childhood. My parents were wonderful people who wanted to give their child a warm and loving home. And I miss them so much." Her voice hitched. "They think I'm dead. I had to convince them of that or they would have spent their life savings looking for me."

"We'll make it safe for you to contact them again—when we bust up this nasty business."

"Just the two of us?"

"No. We need help."

"We can't go to the police or the FBI. Who would believe the story I've just told you?"

"The Light Street Detective Agency. They've handled some pretty strange cases. Nothing is beyond the realm of possibility for them."

"Light Street. That's where you used to work. You would trust them with this?"

"Yes."

When she relaxed a little, he put a hand to her chin, tipping her head up so that his lips could meet hers.

At first, she went very still, then she responded to him, and he felt a surge of unexpected emotions. Not so long ago, he had been sure she was playing him for a fool. Now his protective instincts surged. He wanted to keep her safe. To...

He couldn't allow himself to go any further. Not when this was all so new. But he could show her with his kiss how much he cared.

He granted himself that pleasure for several moments, and when she matched his passion, he felt his heart leap. He wanted to make love to her. To prove that her being a clone had nothing to do with his view of her. He saw her as a warm, loving, courageous woman. Nothing more or less. And he wanted her to believe that. But it wasn't safe to focus on the two of them. Not yet.

Lifting his head, he asked, "From what you've said, I gather you think the Paladin's men are the ones after us?"

She nodded.

"We need to contact Light Street right away, but I can't risk using my cell again." He found a phone on the wall in the kitchen and picked up the receiver. The line was disconnected, probably because the people who owned the cabin didn't want to pay for service when they weren't here.

"We'll have to find a store where I can buy a prepaid phone. Get dressed," he told Grace.

"We borrowed a bed from the homeowners. We should wash the sheets."

He laughed. "We're running late. We'll send them new sheets when we have the time."

They both hurried back to the bedroom.

"Do we have time to take a shower?"

"A quick one."

They each ducked into a separate bathroom, where they showered, then used the tooth-brushes he'd bought and pulled on the cloth-ing from the same discount department store. After they were dressed, he rummaged in the closet and found hats for both of them.

"Put this on," he said, handing her a baseball cap with the logo of a local team.

She winced. "You think the Paladin's goons can find us?"

"No. But I don't want to take any chances."

A KNOCK AT THE office door made Ian Wickers glance up. "Come in."

Phil Yarborough stepped into the room look-ing as if he'd been up all night, tracking down leads. Which he had been. A few hours ago he'd reported that Karen Hilliard had died in an explosion in a house in Frederick. Now she wasn't going to be telling anyone what she'd done to John Ridgeway. And who was helping her. Or whom she was working for. Ian didn't know the answer to either. And now he never would.

"Have you found out what happened to Brady Lockwood?" the Ridgeway chief of security asked.

"No. But it turns out he was probably seen at a hospital in Frederick—near where that house exploded. After that, he's disappeared off the face of the earth."

"What was he being treated for?"

"He left before they got his personal information. But the guy we think is him came in with smoke inhalation."

"Which makes me think he's in this up to his eyeballs. He was part of a conspiracy to kill his brother. Then he knocked off one of the witnesses. But I'm still wondering, did he have the resources to get Hilliard out of custody?"

Yarborough shrugged. "You want to alert the FBI to Lockwood's possible involvement?"

"Let me think about that." Wickers shifted in his seat. "What about the other woman— Grace Cunningham?"

"A woman who fits her description was seen with Lockwood at the hospital. I think we can assume they're together. Which makes it pretty damn certain that they were in it together."

"Keep looking for both of them."

BRADY HURRIED Grace out of the house.

"Where are we going?" she asked when they were back in the car.

"There ought to be a shopping center close by where we can get a phone."

"Okay."

He headed for Martinsburg, thinking that they were taking a chance sticking with the same stolen car, but he was willing to risk it because they could ditch the vehicle as soon as the Light Street men picked them up.

Of course, it was still a little inconvenient

that he had to cross a couple of wires every time he wanted to start the engine.

Beside him, Grace cleared her throat. "You've heard of nature versus nurture?"

"Yeah."

"Environment is part of what makes a person who he or she is."

"What's your point?"

"I know John Ridgeway was ruthless. But Kevin is more balanced. Because of the Parsons, the people who raised him."

He sighed. "And Karen?"

"She had a good home, too. But she was pretty angry when she discovered what Cortez had done to her. It made her start contacting the rest of us. And then when she found out about what your brother was planning for Kevin, she was determined not to let it happen."

"Yeah, John was great at righteous indignation. She got that from him."

"Enough so that in this case, she was pretty sure she wasn't going to survive. I mean, she never said that to me, but we both knew it."

"You were in a pretty shaky position, too."

"Yes. But I told myself I could get away. I couldn't have done it without you." She reached over and laid her hand over his. "But you're free to get out—while the getting's good."

He turned his hand up so he could press his fingers against hers. "In the first place, I'm in too deeply to quit. In the second place, I'm not leaving you."

"Thanks," she whispered.

He found a drugstore and pulled into a space near the door but left the engine running.

"You stay here. I'll be right back as soon as I can."

It took only a few minutes to buy the phone. While he was still inside, he called the familiar Light Street number.

Max Dakota answered.

"Hey, long time no see," he said as soon as he heard Brady's voice. He paused for a moment. "I heard about your brother. I'm sorry."

"Yeah. Thanks," he answered. He didn't want to say too much over the phone, but he needed to let them know that the situation was urgent. "I've been investigating his death, and I've gotten into a situation. I'm going to need some help."

Max didn't ask any questions besides, "What do you need?"

Brady hesitated for a moment, then added a bit more information. "His people are covering something up. Something big that I stumbled on to. I'm in Martinsburg, West Virginia, and I need you to pick up me and a woman."

"You're hiding out?"

"At the moment, I'm at a shopping center." He gave the location.

"Sit tight. We'll get there as soon as we can. Let me have your number."

After giving the number, he returned to the car and saw relief wash over Grace's face. "I was starting to worry."

"Sorry. I wanted to call the Light Street guys as soon as possible."

She nodded and swiped a hand through her

hair. "I'm going to meet your friends, and I feel like a mess."

"You're fine."

Ignoring him, she pointed to a cheap department store like the one where he'd bought the clothes they were wearing. "Would you mind if I bought some fresh underwear?"

"Sounds like a good plan. Get me a package, too."

"What size?"

He gave her the specs as he drove to the other end of the parking lot where they would be close to the store entrance. "This time, I'll wait for you."

"I'll be quick."

He slouched down in the seat, watching her disappear into the long, low building.

Moments after she stepped inside, a black car pulled up in the parking lot. He felt a zing of alarm go through him as soon as he saw the vehicle. It looked like one of the ones from Frederick. But how could that be? No, it had to be a coincidence.

Still he kept his gaze fixed on the vehicle as it pulled into a parking space. And his breath caught when two of the men who had kidnapped him and Grace got out. Both of them were wearing jackets, but he could see the bulk of pistols underneath them.

One of them was holding something in his hand. It could have been a cell phone, but he was staring down at it as if he was watching the screen.

They headed straight into the building without even glancing at the cars in the parking lot—as if they knew exactly where to find what they were looking for.

But how?

A jolt of insight almost cut off his breath. That thing under Grace's skin. It must be more than a serial number. It was a transmitter.

Cursing under his breath, he cut off the engine and got out of the car, ducking low in case there was still someone in the car watching the parking lot. Pulling his cap down over his eyes, he hunched his shoulders and hurried toward the door.

Grace had said she was going to buy underwear. That meant she was in the women's department. Hell! He'd asked for underwear, too. And she could be there instead.

Still cursing under his breath, he stepped into the building, which wasn't crowded.

Too bad it wasn't empty because innocent people could get hurt. Or were these guys smart enough not to start shooting in a public area?

Brady wanted to rush down the nearest aisle. Instead he studied the overhead signs as he tried to get his bearings. The men's and women's departments were both on the same side of the building, which made his job a little easier.

But he needed to make a stop in the drugstore section, too.

He was wondering which route to take when he saw the two men heading purposefully toward the women's department.

Yeah, that was the way to do it. Let them find Grace.

And then what?

He didn't know, but he picked up a heavy saucepan as he walked through the housewares department. Too bad his gun was long gone.

A woman pushing a shopping cart eyed him, then gave him a wide berth. He didn't blame her. He probably looked like a guy out to commit assault.

He stayed behind the thugs, hoping they wouldn't turn around. When they all rounded a corner, he spotted Grace, who stopped in her tracks when she saw the goons bearing down on her.

Brady dashed forward and slammed the pot down on one of the guy's heads. He dropped like a stone in a pond.

But the other one whirled, reaching for the gun under his jacket.

Before he could draw it, Grace gave the shopping cart she was wheeling a hard push, slamming it into the guy's back and knocking him off his feet.

"Go down the left cross aisle, and I'll meet you," Brady yelled, glancing around. Lucky for them, nobody had come upon the melee. But the guy who'd gone down from the blow to his head had gotten up again. The guy was unsteady on his feet. When he lunged forward, Brady grabbed the device from his hand, smashed the screen against a metal shelf, then pushed the guy into a pantyhose display before catching up with Grace at the next corner.

"How did they find us?" she panted.

"That thing under your arm must be sending out a signal."

She gasped.

"I smashed the locator, but they could have another one in the car. We've got to get the thing out from under your skin." Sparing a glance behind them, he led her toward the medicine aisle and grabbed a bottle of alcohol off of a shelf, then a bag of cotton balls and some tape and sterile pads.

Next he sprinted into the cosmetics section where he snatched up cuticle scissors.

When he heard footsteps approaching rapidly, he looked up to see that one of the thugs was on his feet and sprinting toward them.

"I'll hold him off. You dig that thing out of your arm, and break it," he shouted as he thrust the supplies toward her.

She made a moaning sound but took the scissors, alcohol and cotton balls and disappeared around the next corner.

With nobody else in the aisle, the man pulled his gun. "Hold it right there."

Brady ducked and began pulling items off the shelf—anything that came to hand—and started throwing them at the gunman.

A bullet whizzed past him, but when he scored a hit to the guy's temple with a metal box, the thug made a grunting sound and raised his hand to his head. It came away covered with blood.

"You bastard."

IN THE NEXT AISLE, Grace frantically dug at the plastic wrapper enclosing the scissors. When she couldn't make a dent in the packing material, she used her teeth to tear through the thick packaging.

Slipping her fingers into the handles of the instrument, she worked the blades.

Was she really going to try and cut the thing out of her arm with cuticle scissors? Was Brady right that the bad guys had found her because she was carrying around some kind of signal beacon?

That made sense, in a kind of horrible way, yet it would require some very sophisticated technology. Cortez couldn't have done it by himself, but he'd probably had a whole range of experts that he could tap for various assignments.

Her inner debate was cut short when she heard a shot ring out from the next aisle. It helped ground her to reality. Brady was fighting for her, and she'd better do her part to make sure the bad guys couldn't follow them out of this store.

If they got out. She couldn't even be sure of that.

She cut off that awful thought.

With her heart pounding, she unbuttoned her shirt and pulled her arm out of the sleeve. After swabbing the area over the disk with alcohol, she poured more alcohol onto the scissors.

Before she could chicken out, she plunged the point of one blade into her arm.

The pain shot along her nerve endings, but she knew she had to keep going. Teeth clenched, she worked to get the metal tip of a scissors blade under the thing that was embedded in her body.

She had to pause to fight a wave of dizziness.

"Stop it," she ordered herself as she got back to work.

When the thing moved under her skin, she used her free hand to keep it in place while she dug with the blade, amazed that she could hold her hands steady.

SNARLING, THE assailant raised the gun again, just as a store employee came around the corner in back of the thug.

"Watch out," Brady shouted.

The thug whirled, and the clerk gasped.

Brady sprang forward, tackling the man with the gun and pulling him to the floor.

"What the hell?" the employee shouted.

"Call the police," Brady answered. "This guy is trying to kidnap my wife."

The clerk backed away, and Brady slammed the thug's face against the tile floor, then did it again for good measure.

When the guy went limp, Brady got up, dodged around the corner and found Grace sitting on the floor, one arm out of the sleeve of her shirt. She was taping a bandage to her arm.

He winced. "You got it out?"

Wordlessly, she held up a small disk that she'd dug from under her skin.

He would have liked to examine the damn thing, but it was too dangerous to keep around. So he held out his hand, and she laid it in his palm. It was light. Probably plastic, but it had to have some circuitry inside.

"Give me the scissors."

When she handed over the instrument, he slipped the disk between the blades and cut it in half. Then he cut it again. Was it safe to keep it, now that it was destroyed? Taking a chance, he slipped the pieces into his pocket.

Grace stood up, wavering on her feet.

"Are you all right?"

"Yes," she answered, but her voice was thin.

"You put alcohol on it?"

"Yes."

He was about to lead her back to the car when he heard a police siren in the distance and knew they had to get out of the store before the cops arrived and started asking questions.

Like why John Ridgeway's brother was on the run.

Which meant they'd better not go back to the stolen car sitting in the parking lot.

"Come on. We can't let the police find us here."

"Why not?"

"That trip down the mountain was designed to set us up as conspirators fleeing from the law. We don't know if they've already put out the story that we're guilty of killing John. Or Karen, for that matter."

Grace nodded, then followed him down the aisle, toward a different door from the one where they'd come in.

Since they'd been in the store, they hadn't seen many customers. But now the people who'd been shopping were streaming toward the exits, along with many of the employees.

Peeking out from behind a rack of men's shirts, Brady watched two cops enter the store by the door they'd originally come in.

"Stay back," he warned Grace.

When the officers had disappeared down an aisle leading to the drugstore area, he grabbed a couple of shirts and handed one to Grace. They huddled between two racks of clothing as he pulled the tabs off the merchandise and dragged his T-shirt off and over his head. Moments later, he was wearing the new shirt.

"Put on that shirt," he told her. "We both have to look different."

While she quickly complied, he reached behind a counter and pulled out a plastic bag.

After thrusting the old shirts and his hat inside, he took Grace's hand as they walked to the exit. Once outside, he pulled her into the crowd of customers milling on the sidewalk.

As they tried to blend with the shoppers, one of the bad guys came running out of the other door, heading for the black car that had appeared after Grace had entered the store. Before the thug reached it, a cop caught up with him and pulled him to a stop. The other guy was just closing the door as the car that had brought him roared away.

"So much for loyalty among kidnappers," Grace murmured.

He sighed.

"What?"

"The car we stole is still here. And my fingerprints are all over the interior."

"Mine, too."

"Are yours on record?"

"I don't think so. I mean, I don't remember being fingerprinted." She hitched in a breath. "Of course, the woman I'm copied from might have been."

"Yeah, right. Do you know who that is?"

She turned away from him and stared straight ahead. He could see the tense set of her jaw.

Did she know who it was?

GRACE SLID HIM a sidewise look. "I'm sorry, but...I don't want to talk about that right now."

"I know the subject's difficult for you."

Changing the subject abruptly, she asked, "Where are we going?"

"Let's act innocent for the time being. Maybe we didn't even see the ruckus in the department store." He led her down the row of shops, toward a fast-food restaurant.

She dragged in a breath and let it out. "That thing—was it working as a tracking device all along?"

He thought about the past eighteen hours. "I don't think it was turned on. Remember, they found us at the hotel because I used my cell phone. And they lured us to the house by getting Karen to phone. They were waiting for us to show up at the house with Karen."

"Then they lost us, and somebody turned it on?"

"That's what I'm assuming."

"But how could they know who I am?"

"Each disk could give off a different signal."

"But...they don't know my real name. It's not Grace Cunningham. They couldn't be looking for *me* explicitly." She stopped walking and grabbed his arm.

"What?"

"If they don't know who I am, maybe they're going after all the clones. I mean, the Paladin's been after *us*. But suppose he's figured out some of the clones are acting together—against him and anybody else who was involved in creating them. Because he doesn't know which ones, he's going after any of us he can find. His men zeroed in on me because they were already in the area."

Brady thought about that. "You may be right."

"If they can find me, they can find Kevin." She held out her hand. "Can I use the phone? I have to warn him."

He glanced around. "There's some chance that they could come back looking for us. We have to get out of here first."

"We can't go near the car."

"Right."

He led her to the end of the strip mall. Beyond it was a wooded area. And beyond that was what looked like the back of another shopping center.

After glancing around, he stepped off the blacktop and onto the grass, then headed for the woods.

GRACE FOLLOWED.

Until they reached the shelter of the trees, she felt terribly exposed. But the shade of the branches reduced her stress level a little.

When they were in the shadows, Brady handed her the phone. "Make it quick. I also need to tell Light Street what happened."

Grace propped her back against a tree trunk and punched in the number. Tension coursed through her as she waited. One, two, three rings. Maybe he wouldn't pick up because he didn't recognize the number.

Four, five, six.

It kicked into voice mail.

"This is Kevin," a chipper voice said, as if he was a high-school student talking to one of his friends. "Leave me a message, and I'll get back to you as soon as I can."

She glanced at Brady. "He's not answering. What should I do?"

"Leave him a message. But don't give too much away."

"Kevin," she said, struggling to keep her voice even, "this is Grace. I'm calling from a prepaid cell phone."

She looked around before continuing. "You know that guy who's been making trouble for us? Some of his men showed up out of the blue at a shopping center where we'd gone to buy some clothing."

Again she stopped, wondering how to phrase the next part. Finally, with no other alternative, she said, "We figured out that…that funny birthmark on your arm is a locating device. You've got to get it out of you. And destroy it."

Brady made a slicing motion with his hand.

Grace read the gesture. "I've got to go. We'll contact you later." She paused. "Stay safe."

After pressing the off button, she handed the phone back.

"He might be avoiding you," Brady said. "He could have been listening to the message and not picking up."

"Why would he do that?"

"Earlier, you told him you were with me? Maybe he doesn't think much of the company you're keeping."

KEVIN PARSONS STARED at the phone. Yesterday when Grace had called him, he'd answered. Now he wasn't sure it was such a good idea.

She was with Brady Lockwood, John Ridgeway's brother. Or so she said.

He couldn't be sure of that. He couldn't even be sure that the two of them weren't being held by the Paladin's men.

He grimaced. A few years ago, he'd had such a normal life. With parents who loved him. He'd always known he was adopted, but that hadn't made any difference in their relationship.

Then he'd been at the Princeton library, researching a paper on relations with Cuba,
when a woman about his age sat down across
the table from him. He glanced up and thought
she looked familiar.

She said she had something important to discuss and asked him to take a walk with her.
What she said had changed his life. Or given
him a chance to live, if you wanted to look at
it a different way.

He was John Ridgeway's clone, which put
him in danger because the bastard who'd com-
missioned him had a heart problem. And Kevin
was his best hope for a complete recovery.

The beauty of it was that once John Ridgeway
got his new heart, he wouldn't have to worry
about taking drugs to prevent organ rejection.
The heart would be completely compatible
with his own body.

And Kevin Parsons would be dead.

He pressed the repeat button and listened to
the message again. Grace sounded sincere. But
he still wasn't sure. She'd told him Karen had

called *her* sounding normal but scared. Then they'd found her drugged out of her mind.

Turning away from the machine, he walked to the window and stared out into the afternoon sun. He was in a beautiful area. The Shenandoah Valley, with the Blue Ridge Mountains in the distance.

He and Karen had found this farm together and rented the property. They'd spent some good times here. Talking to her had been an amazing experience. She was so much like him—yet with a feminine point of view that he sometimes found startling.

And now she was dead.

Throwing back his head, he let a long scream of pain flow from his mouth. He had cherished her in a way few people could appreciate. Maybe identical twins who had been separated at birth would understand. Nobody else. And she had sacrificed herself for him. He hadn't thought it would turn out that way. Now he knew he'd been fooling himself. She'd wanted to get John Ridgeway—no matter what happened to her.

He wanted revenge. Was it possible to get it by himself, or did he need Grace and Brady Lockwood? And why would Brady Lockwood want to help his brother's clone?

Well, first things first. He'd better have a look at the thing under his arm.

GRACE LISTENED AS Brady called the Light Street Detective Agency and quickly filled them in on developments. From the conversation, she knew that he trusted these men implicitly. She hoped that he was right—and that Light Street could get to them in time, although she didn't exactly know what "in time" meant.

"I'll see if we can find a nearby fast-food restaurant to wait," Brady said.

When the person on the other end of the line questioned his decision, he laughed. "You think maybe Grace and I should climb into a Dumpster?"

Again he waited for a reply, then said, "How long will it take to get here?"

When he clicked off, she asked, "How long?"

"They're already on their way. About forty-five minutes to an hour." He gave her a critical look. "You just had a minor operation. You need to sit."

Near the end of the row of shops was a place called Palo's Pizza.

"A pizza parlor is as good as anywhere else," he said.

"I'd like a nice dark movie theater better."

None was around so they stepped into the pizza parlor. It was a long, narrow room with some tables in front and along one wall. The service counter was about twelve feet from the front door, and a hallway at the back led to restrooms and a phone. Because it was still a couple of hours before lunchtime, the only people here were the two men behind the counter and a couple at the only occupied table.

"Get a table," he told her. "I'm going to see if there's a back way out."

She headed for the tables along the wall and sat down, feeling more wrung out than she'd admitted to Brady.

Brady walked toward the restrooms and kept going. A few minutes later, he was back without the bag he'd taken from the department store. "There's a door at the end of the hall that leads to a parking area. We can go out that way, if we need to. Beyond that's more woods. So I think we're in good shape." He glanced toward the counter. "Now for some food."

He ordered for them, then joined her at the table.

"You watch the front, and I'll watch the back," he said.

At first they both kept glancing at the doors, but gradually they relaxed a little.

"I feel like I've been on the run for days," she murmured after she'd chewed a bite of pizza.

"More like years," he answered. "I guess it

was pretty hard cutting yourself off from your family."

"Yes. But it's best for them." Changing the subject, she asked, "Where did you grow up?"

"My mom moved us to San Jose, California, when she got a job at a software company."

"Did you like living there?"

"It was okay."

"What did you do for fun?"

When he thought he saw a flash of movement on the sidewalk out front, his gaze flicked to the front door. But it was apparently nothing. Focusing on Grace again, he said, "The usual. Played sports. Went to the movies. Hung out with the guys at the mall." He laughed. "And I was a comic-book fiend."

She smiled. "I was more into girl stuff. Maybe because that's what my parents expected. I had a lot of dolls when I was little. Then I hit my teens and got into clothing. When I look back on that, it seems so superficial."

"No. It was normal."

She changed the subject back to him. "You didn't see your brother much?"

"I spent some summers with his family in New Jersey. He and I didn't get together much until after—"

He stopped, and she didn't press him. She was pretty sure he'd been about to say *"after Carol and Lisa died."*

She took another drag on her cola. As they sat facing each other, the pizza grew cold and less appealing, but they both made the meal last because staying in here was safer than going outside.

"We didn't have a luxurious lifestyle. I guess my mother could have made me hate the Ridgeways, but she never bad-mouthed them. That's why I could get together with John... later."

She nodded, but her mind was zinging back to their current problem. "You think the cops got all the bad guys?"

"Well, that car pulled away. So we know at least one of them escaped."

She tightened her fingers around her paper cup. She'd wanted to hear him say that they were safe, but he was too honest for that. When she saw that she was crushing the cup, she eased up on the pressure.

"I feel like I have a target on my back," she finally said.

"Yeah, but there are no good choices because we've got to stick around here. The cops could still be looking for the couple who were involved in the disturbance. If they find us in the woods, they won't think we're taking a nature hike. If we start walking down the highway, we're going to stand out. And going back to a stolen car is definitely out. There's some chance the cops even think the thugs arrived in it."

"But the black car drove off when the guy ran for it."

"They don't know where the man on foot was running."

"I guess you consider all the angles."

"My detective's mind."

She leaned back in her seat and took another bite of pizza. The other customers had left, and they were alone in the restaurant with the men at the counter.

He looked over his shoulder to make sure they were alone and asked, "How many…individuals did Cortez make?"

"Karen might have had that information, but I don't know."

"How long did she spend locating them?"

"A couple of years."

"How many people are in the organization she put together?" he asked.

"I don't know." She raised one shoulder. "I guess it sounds like I'm pretty uninformed for someone who was willing to get in so deep."

"You had your reasons."

"Karen set up cells. We didn't all know each other."

He lowered his voice. "So you only worked with Karen and her brother?"

"Basically."

She was thinking that they had to find the

Paladin and get to his list of the others when the front door opened. As she looked up, she froze. It was one of the men who had followed them into the department store.

# Chapter Thirteen

Brady followed Grace's gaze. Cursing under his breath, he stood. He'd made a determination that it was safer staying here than other places he could have chosen. Apparently, he'd been wrong. Or maybe there were enough bad guys looking for them that it didn't matter where they'd gone—as long as they were still in the area. But at least they had an escape route out the back way.

Or he'd thought so until Grace turned back toward him and went rigid, her gaze focused behind him.

Pretty sure of what he was going to see, he

shifted to look over his shoulder, where he saw another one of the bad guys had come in the back door and was advancing toward them.

They were sandwiched between the two thugs, and it looked as if there was no way out, unless they could find a trapdoor in the floor.

The man who had come in the front walked over to their table. He'd been holding a gun down beside his leg, where the men at the counter couldn't see it. When he was a few feet from them, he lifted his arm and pointed the weapon at them.

His face turned smug as he ordered, "Come on."

"You're not going to start shooting in here."

"Don't bet on it."

Brady glanced at the counter where the two men had been working. They'd both ducked out of sight. Maybe they'd get a chance to call the cops—which could be good or bad, depending on how this went down.

Brady stood slowly. Grace did the same. Her

face was white but determined, and he knew she wasn't going to go quietly.

The pizza he'd managed to eat congealed in his stomach. What if she preferred death to capture?

"Out the back. Get moving."

Taking a chance, Brady put his hands on the table as though his knees had gone weak, and he needed to steady himself.

"Come on," the gunman growled.

Brady moved, shouting "Duck" as he picked up the table and used it to shield himself while he threw it at the guy who was coming in from the front.

The flat surface hit the man, knocking him backward. Grace moved at the same time, snatching up a sugar canister from the table and hurling it at the other thug.

He fired, but she had already scooted to the side, and the slug went into the wall.

The first guy was getting up, but Brady bashed him over the head with a chair. Blood from a scalp wound pooled on the tile floor, and Brady had the fleeting thought that it was going to be hard for the restaurant guys to clean up.

When he turned, the other thug was sprawled at Grace's feet with sugar scattered around him.

"That felt good," she murmured.

"Yeah."

One of the men behind the counter was peering over the edge.

"They're down?"

"Yeah."

"I'll call the cops."

Brady wanted to tell them not to, but that wasn't going to make any sense to a guy who had just watched two customers fight off an attack from armed intruders.

"We've got to get out of here," he said to Grace in a low voice.

"Hey, man, you can't leave," the man shouted.

Instead of answering, Brady turned to Grace. "Come on."

"Which way? Front or back?"

He considered the question. If they went out the front, they'd have to hustle to get away from the cops.

If they went out the back, a big black car could be waiting to take them away. To their deaths. But maybe the driver was the one lying on the floor with his head bleeding.

Bending down, he took the gun from the guy's hand. "Out the back," he said, covering the door as they approached.

They stepped into the rear parking area, and he tensed when he saw the car. But nobody was behind the wheel. Apparently there had only been two thugs, and they were both out cold in the restaurant.

Opening the car door, he saw that the keys were in the ignition.

"Get in," he said to Grace.

"The last time—"

He cut her off. "But they drove here. The brakes must have been working."

"Or the car's going to explode when you turn the key."

He made a low sound. She could be right. The way things were playing out, this could be another death trap. In which case, he didn't want anyone else getting blown up.

Reaching inside, he carefully extracted the keys from the ignition and tossed them into the Dumpster beside the front door.

Once again, he heard the sound of police sirens. He and Grace were already fugitives. If they got caught now, with two guys out cold on the floor of the restaurant, it was going to be a lot worse.

As he evaluated their chances of getting away, he knew the woods were the only option.

"Hurry." Grabbing Grace's hand, he took off in that direction, praying they could make it before the cops came charging out the back door of the restaurant.

When they reached the trees, Grace dragged in a deep breath and let it out as she leaned against a tree. "We made it."

"I hope. Move around the tree, so it's between you and the back of the strip mall."

She slid around the trunk, and he did the same.

Easing his head out, he looked back toward the rear of the restaurant in time to see an officer striding toward the car.

"We'd better put some distance between us and the cops."

As they both turned and made tracks, he pulled out his cell phone and called Light Street again.

"Change of plans. The bad guys showed up at the pizza parlor where we were eating. We're crossing a wooded area in back of the shopping center."

"Not to worry," came the answer from Max Dakota. He was silent for a few moments, then said, "Livestock Market Road is on the other side of the woods. Head for the road. We'll detour and pick you up."

"Thanks."

As they pushed on through the trees, Brady muttered, "Sorry."

"For what?"

"We should have cleared out of the area instead of holing up in a restaurant."

"You made the best determination you could. You wanted a place where I could sit down. And if we had started down the road, they might have scooped us up with no chance to get away."

She was right, of course, but he still felt guilty.

They ran until they reached the far edge of the woods and stopped short. A police car was pulled up along the shoulder.

Brady cursed under his breath.

"How did they find us?"

"The cop must have spotted us go in. Or they could have come this way because it was a logical escape route."

"What are we going to do?"

He thought fast. "We can't retrace our steps. We'll have to go parallel to the road."

They moved cautiously to the side and kept going, picking up their pace. But Brady suspected they weren't putting enough distance between themselves and the patrol car.

Looking in back of him, he saw another cop car hugging the woods, closing in on them.

He was thinking they weren't going to make it when a series of explosions split the air.

Brady grabbed Grace and threw her to the ground, rolling on top of her. They lay wedged together as two more concussions banged against them.

"What's happening? Was that the car?" she breathed when the noise and vibrations stopped.

"Don't know. It's not aimed at us, I think."

He could hear running feet and looked up in time to see the officer out of his car. He was taking off toward a farmhouse on the other side of the road.

"We'd better get out of here while we can."

He rolled to his side and was about to stand

up when he saw someone striding toward him through the woods.

It took a moment to recognize Hunter Kelley, who was dressed like a farmer who'd just come in from plowing the fields.

"You change professions?" Brady asked as he got to his feet.

"No. I'm trying to look like I live in West Virginia. This way."

He led them back the way they'd come, circling around the cop car.

"What were the explosions?" Brady asked.

Hunter laughed. "Must have been some kids setting off fireworks at that vacant house down the road."

"Yeah, right."

"Grace Cunningham—Hunter Kelley, from the Light Street Detective Agency," Brady said.

"Nice to meet you," they both answered.

A car pulled onto the road from a side lane, and they climbed into the backseat.

Max Dakota was at the wheel. "I see you

can't stay out of trouble," he commented as he pulled away, driving at a moderate pace. Once again, Brady made introductions.

Sitting back, he took a deep breath, allowing himself to relax for the first time since he'd met Grace outside her apartment.

Ten minutes later, the car turned into a field where a helicopter was waiting.

Grace goggled at it. "You came in *that?*"

"Faster than driving here from Western Maryland."

"That's where the Randolph Security test labs are located," Brady explained to Grace. "Randolph and Light Street are sister companies. We work together on an as-needed basis."

They climbed out of the car, and Brady helped Grace into a seat on the chopper and handed her a pair of earphones with a microphone attached. "It's going to be noisy," he said. "If you need to speak, you can use the comms unit."

They took off as soon as they were belted

in, but both he and Grace were silent on the trip from Martinsburg. There was no point in starting a conversation now, because they would have to repeat it as soon as they got to the Randolph facility.

By helicopter it was only a forty-five-minute ride to the secure lab. As soon as the chopper landed, Brady sighed. He'd half expected a guided missile to come streaking at the helicopter. Now they were safely on the ground, and no one could reach them here. However, they had a lot of explaining to do.

These people had come to their rescue with no questions asked. They were about to find out some inconvenient facts.

After helping Grace down, he turned to see a dozen colleagues he'd worked with before he went out on his own. Hunter's wife, Kathryn Kelley, was there. As well as husband and wife Jo O'Malley and Cameron Randolph, who owned The Light Street Detective Agency and Randolph Security, respectively.

Thorn Devereaux, Jed Prentiss, Max Dakota, and Nick Vickers also joined the group.

"We were sorry to hear about your brother," Jed said.

"It's complicated," Brady clipped out, then glanced at Kathryn Kelley. She was a psychologist, and she probably saw the tension coursing through him.

When Grace hung back, he brought her forward, introducing her to the crowd. But he could see she was on edge. He knew these people. She was stepping into an unfamiliar situation, and what she was going to say wouldn't put her in a very flattering light. But he'd help her through it.

"Why don't we get comfortable in the lounge," Kathryn said, and he was grateful for the reprieve.

In the lounge, everyone got something to drink. Nothing alcoholic, which he suspected was for his benefit. They all knew what had happened to him after Carol and Lisa had died.

Brady reached for Grace's hand, and she knit her fingers with his. He gave her a reassuring squeeze before saying, "I found out after my brother's death that he was involved in a very nasty scheme to provide him with spare parts if he needed them."

"You mean an illegal organ-donor program?" Jo asked. A long time ago, she'd helped break up a ring that was providing organs to wealthy customers.

"You could say that," Brady answered. Deciding to spell it out before they got any further, he added, "In this case, John was going to get a new heart from a young man who was his clone. A man who was adopted and raised by foster parents who weren't clued in that he'd been created specifically for the purpose of providing backup organs for John Ridgeway. Of course, he didn't have a clue, either."

There were exclamations around the room.

"How do you know?" Hunter Kelley asked with an edge in his voice.

Brady had known Hunter would react to the news more than the others.

"One of the clones found out about the secret project that produced her. She broke into the records of the laboratory and got the names of some others, and they vowed to join together to protect themselves. When they learned that John was getting ready to have a heart transplant, they came up with a scheme to eliminate him before he could kill his clone."

For a moment, nobody spoke. Then Grace cleared her throat, and everyone looked at her. She sat rigidly in her seat, and he pressed her hand again.

"The news accounts said John Ridgeway was alone when he died. But that's part of what his security men are covering up. Ridgeway was having an affair with a woman, and his chief of security didn't want the great man's image tarnished with the sordid details of an affair. His paramour's name was Karen Hilliard. I was her lookout because all of us vowed to help protect the others."

She raised her chin. "I'm one of the clones."

Hunter cleared his throat. "If you think we haven't heard about clones being raised for un-ethical purposes, you're wrong. That was ex-actly my role. So I understand where you're coming from."

Grace gasped as she stared at him. "You're saying *you're* a clone, too?"

"Exactly," he answered. "But I was supposed to be the perfect assassin. I'd go on a mission to the Middle East, and they wouldn't have to worry about getting me back." He looked at his wife. "Kathryn rescued me. We're married, and we have a son. Your background doesn't mean you can't lead a normal life."

Grace nodded wordlessly, obviously shocked by the revelation and probably relieved that this group of people had already accepted a man who was a clone. Still, her next words sent a chill down his spine.

"Of course, that doesn't excuse the fact that I was involved in a murder plot."

Brady watched the reactions around the

room. He knew Grace had made the claim for shock value, and he wasn't going to let her get away with it.

"You agreed to help Karen Hilliard go after John Ridgeway because he was going to kill his clone for spare parts."

"Does that excuse killing him?"

"It was a case of kill or be killed," Brady answered.

"We felt that way," Grace answered. "We swore to protect any one of us who was going to be…harvested."

"Tell them how Karen Hilliard found out about the secret lab that produced her," Brady prompted.

"Because she was also John Ridgeway's clone."

In response to the looks of confusion and shock around the room, Brady went on to explain about Dr. Cortez and his unconscionable experiments.

"How did you find out you were part of the program?" Jed gently asked Grace.

She took a moment before answering. "When Karen came to me and told me I was the clone of a millionaire's daughter, I didn't believe her. But then the clone of an oil executive was sacrificed. And after that it was a diplomat. Because I couldn't deny the evidence, I went into hiding. And I had plastic surgery, so I wouldn't look like my...original."

"Can you give us some names of people who sacrificed their clones?" Max asked.

She nodded. "William Swatson. Donald Henderson."

Brady sucked in a sharp breath. "I remember when Swatson was in the hospital."

"Yeah. And unfortunately, there have been others since." She gave them the names of a governor, a drug-company executive, a football player, a woman news anchor.

"What about the millionaire's daughter?" Jo asked.

Grace glanced at Brady. "I should have told you already. I was working up my nerve to say—it's Barbara Frazier."

"Barbara Frazier," Brady choked out. "The wife of Patrick Frazier, who was in line to take over as CEO of the Ridgeway Consortium?"

"Yes."

He considered the implications. "She hated John." He paused, thinking he should rephrase that statement. "Well, I guess it wasn't personal. She thought her husband should be head of the Ridgeway Consortium. I've heard her talking about how much better qualified he was. It wasn't true, and there was no way he was going to get the job—as long as John was alive."

Grace nodded in agreement. "Yes. She was ambitious for her husband, and she was willing to do what it took to advance his position."

Brady listened in disbelief. He'd never liked Barbara, but he hadn't considered her a danger to his brother.

"I told you Karen Hilliard and I met John Ridgeway at a party." Grace dragged in a breath and let it out. "It was Barbara's party."

"How did Karen know Barbara?" Brady asked.

"Karen started going to that fancy restaurant where Barbara likes to have lunch. They got to talking, and Karen told her it was a shame her husband had to play second fiddle to John Ridgeway. From there, it was a short step to hatching a plot. She helped us get to Ridgeway because she wanted him out of the way." Grace looked at Brady. "I'm sorry."

"No, I needed to know about it."

"And Barbara's fingerprints *are* probably on record."

He laughed. "Then the cops will wonder what she was doing in a stolen junk car in West Virginia."

Grace nodded.

"Let me tell the story from here," he said.

She leaned back against the sofa cushions. He was sure she wanted to be alone, but she stayed beside him.

"You might remember that the man who produced the clones, Dr. Richard Cortez, was blown up, along with his lab," Brady said. "But he wasn't in charge of running the organ-donor phase of the operation. That's a guy we know only as the Paladin. At first I thought Ian Wickers, my brother's security chief, was after us. Maybe he is. But I think the man who's been trying to kill us is this Paladin guy. He wants to make sure we can't tell anyone about the clone program. And he wanted to pin John's death on me—because that would be a plausible alternative to what really happened."

He gave them a condensed version of what they'd been doing over the past few days.

"You're lucky to be alive," Kathryn said when he finished.

"I wouldn't be, without Brady," Grace said. "He's been my bodyguard since the Paladin's men came after me."

He glanced at her, then continued. "We're safe here now. Unfortunately, we're not the only ones in danger. He apparently has a transmitter in every clone. I believe he's figured out that some of them are looking for him, but he doesn't know which ones. From the little I know about him, I'm betting his solution is to wipe all of them out before they can get him."

"Nice guy," Hunter muttered.

"You have a transmitter in you? Can he track you here?" Cam Randolph asked.

"No. It's not in me anymore. After Brady figured out how they found me, I dug it out of my arm."

Kathryn winced. "Do you need medical attention?"

"Probably some more antiseptic. And a fresh bandage," Grace answered.

Brady stood and reached into his pocket. Feeling around, he located the pieces of the transmitter and fished them out, laying them flat in his hand. "Here it is. I figured cutting it up would disable it."

"I'll want to have a look at them in the lab," Cam said. "There may be some new technology involved that I'd like to know about."

Brady passed the pieces over.

"I'm hoping you can help us find the Paladin

and stop him from killing any more innocent people," Brady said to the group.

He glanced at Grace, then back to the others. "And I want to make sure that nobody is hunting Grace."

"We'll give you anything you need," Jo said, then asked, "How did the Paladin get the victims away from their families?"

"Various ways," Grace answered. "Sometimes it looked like they'd run away. Or they died in an accident where the body couldn't be found. You'd be surprised how many options there are to make a body disappear."

Brady took up the story again. "The Paladin always acted as a gatekeeper, deciding who could sacrifice a clone and who couldn't. Apparently he'd denied John's request for a heart transplant, so John tricked me into locating his clone."

"His name is Kevin Parsons," Grace said. "I'm hoping we can bring him here, where he'll be safe."

"He may not agree," Brady said in a gritty voice.

"Why not?" Max asked.

Brady answered, "Because I know my brother. He could be too stubborn to cooperate." He swallowed, "And because he could think I want revenge."

"You don't!" Grace insisted.

"He may have to be convinced of that."

"Whatever his feelings, I hope we can demonstrate that it's to his advantage to work with us," Max muttered.

Brady nodded. A plan was starting to form in his mind. A plan that would require Kevin's cooperation. But he wasn't going to start laying it out yet—not until he talked to Kevin.

"What about the transmitter that's in *his* arm?" Cam Randolph asked.

"I warned him about it. I hope he removed it," Grace said, then gave them a pleading look. "Even with Ridgeway dead and the transmitter removed, Kevin may be in danger. If Brady found him for Ridgeway, the Paladin may be able to find him, too."

"He was in a college dorm when I located him," Brady said. "He's in hiding now."

"It may be harder now," Hunter said. "But we have to make finding Kevin a priority."

"Where do we look?" Cam asked.

"I only have a cell-phone number," Grace answered. "Last time I called him, I got voice mail. He's being cautious about answering, but I'm assuming that he's somewhere not too far from DC."

"Leave him another message."

"He didn't respond to me last time. What should I say?"

They all discussed the options and settled on a script.

When Brady handed her the phone, she called the number, getting voice mail again.

As per instructions, she was more direct than she had been on the previous occasion.

"Kevin, I'm still with Brady Lockwood. We're in a secure location with colleagues of his. I know that you have the file on him. You can look up the Light Street Detective Agency and see that they're very good—and very good at keeping confidential information."

She paused for a moment, hoping he'd pick up, but she was still talking to his voice mail. "I want to bring you here so we can make some plans. You and I aren't the only ones in danger. Our enemy has a list of others he's going after. Please call me back at this number."

After clicking off, she sat very still, hoping that he would decide it was safe to answer.

## Chapter Fourteen

When the phone didn't ring, Brady shook his head. "John was always cautious. And mistrustful, come to that. I think we've got to hope he thinks through his situation and contacts you."

Cam gave him and Grace an appraising look. "Both of you need to decompress. Why don't we all get some rest and reconvene in three hours? Unless we hear from him sooner."

There were nods of agreement around the room.

"We have overnight facilities here," Cam told Grace, "because some of our researchers stay for extended periods. And we've also had guests who needed a place to hide out."

Brady stood up. "I guess you'd better tell us which rooms are free." He glanced at Grace. "After we check out the hole in her arm."

They went to the infirmary, where Brady got out antiseptic. Carefully, he removed the dressing that Grace had slapped over her wound.

"It's healing fine," he said as he inspected her skin. "No infection. You did a good job."

Jed, who had come with them, agreed. He gave Grace an admiring look. "You took that thing out yourself?"

"Yes. But I didn't have any choice."

"You could have chickened out," Brady said as he replaced the dressing with a flat, waterproof one.

Their next stop was a room that could have been part of a small department store. One side had racks and shelves of women's clothes in various sizes. The men's section was smaller, but adequate.

"Grab a couple of outfits," Brady told Grace,

then got himself some jeans and T-shirts, along with the underwear they hadn't had a chance to buy.

He smiled as he watched Grace make a careful selection. Even when they were on the run, women had to think about clothing.

Looking up, she saw both men watching her. "What?"

"Take your time."

"I'm finished," she answered, snatching up a dark blue T-shirt.

With the clothing selections finished, Jed led them down a corridor to the bedroom wing.

"Are you staying together?" he asked.

When Grace hesitated, Brady answered the question with a decisive yes.

Jed led them to a room, then left them.

They stepped into a comfortable space that looked like a room in an upscale hotel. There was a queen-size bed, a bureau, a flat-creen television—and a luxurious bathroom with a spa tub, a shower and an array of designer toiletries.

"I can't believe this place," Grace said, her voice a bit shaky as she set her clothing on the dresser. "It's not like any research facility I've ever heard of."

"Cam and Jo's guests have often had…shall we say, harrowing experiences. They need to relax." He was happy she'd have a chance to pamper herself, if only for a few hours. "I think we should take advantage of their hospitality."

But she looked overwhelmed and unsure of herself.

"What's wrong?" he asked.

"I told you a lot of stuff that must be hard to digest," she said in a low voice.

"Not as hard as you think," he answered.

"You haven't had time to absorb it all. I mean, I could tell how much you hate Barbara Frazier."

"You're not her."

"A lot of people would say I am." She swallowed hard. "Actually, I was horrified to find out who I was."

He reached for her and folded her into his

arms as he murmured, "Are you worried that I'm going to turn away from you because I can't see the difference between you and Barbara Frazier?"

She answered with a small nod.

"You're nothing like her," he repeated, stroking her back and shoulders.

"I have the same genes."

"Yeah, well, didn't you give me a lecture on nature versus nurture? She was raised by parents who kept telling her that she wasn't good enough."

"How do you know?"

"John talked about her. And I did some research of my own because one of my jobs was keeping tabs on Ridgeway Consortium employees and their families."

"Nice."

"John was cautious. Like Kevin, remember."

She nodded.

"The parents who raised you were thrilled to get you and happy with their daughter. They didn't give you the nasty, angry edge that she has. You have all her good traits and none of the bad ones. You're smart and sexy and resourceful. You care about other people—otherwise, you wouldn't have agreed to Karen's plan. But you don't have Barbara's blinding ambition and her absolute disregard for anyone but herself."

"You're sure?"

"Absolutely."

"Being with her gave me a sick feeling."

"It would give anybody the willies to be with the person who'd bought you to have you killed if necessary. I assume she didn't know who you were."

"I didn't tell her, of course. But even though I'd had the plastic surgery, sometimes she used to give me strange looks."

"Yeah, when I first met you, I thought I knew you. Just like I thought I knew Karen. It's the eyes."

"I guess I should have worn contacts to change the color." She sighed. "I thought that after I faked my death and had the surgery, I was safe. I was wrong. I wasn't safe until you told me about that transmitter."

He tightened his arms around her. "I'm not going to let anything happen to you."

As he held her, he tried to imagine what her life must have been like over the past few years. She'd gone from feeling warm and secure with her family to hiding out because she was a marked woman. And she'd made a commitment to saving herself and others from the fiends who had come up with the clever idea of growing human beings for spare parts.

Human beings. Well, that obviously wasn't the way Dr. Cortez—or the Paladin—thought about the babies produced.

Anger bubbled inside Brady. Anger at the way the plan had been conceived and carried out with no regard for whom they hurt. Not only were the clones expendable, but their parents were destined for heartbreak when their children were taken from them.

In a soothing voice, he told her, "You need to unwind. Why don't you start with a hot shower." He led her into the bathroom and turning on the water. "Just get in there and relax," he murmured.

When he'd adjusted the temperature, he went back to the bedroom and closed the door, waiting while she took off her clothes and stepped under the running water. As he stood outside the bathroom, he was trying to imagine what it would do to you to find out that you were a copy of another person. That was bad enough, but the reason you'd been created was even worse. You'd feel as if you were worthless. But he wanted her to know how much he valued her. And he wanted her to know that now.

Fighting not to let arousal give his intentions away, he took off his clothing, then went into the bathroom and stepped inside the shower.

Grace had been lathering her hair with lavender-scented shampoo. She looked up, startled, then she relaxed a little when she saw it was him.

"What are you doing here?" she asked.

He kept his voice conversational. "I was

listening to the shower, and I couldn't help thinking how wonderful it would feel to step under the hot water and have the steam swirling around me."

"Yes, it's good. I feel like I've been cold for days."

The comment was revealing. Yeah, they'd both been out in the cold, and he was going to make sure that she was warm and comfortable for the rest of her life. As soon as they got rid of a few little problems.

She rinsed the shampoo out of her hair, then moved over to give him room under the water.

Losing the battle to keep his body from betraying him, he had to step in back of her where she couldn't see the erection.

"Now that I'm here, let me enjoy myself." He reached for the soap and lathered his hands. Still standing behind her, he stroked his slick fingers over her shoulders, up her neck, around the curves of her ears.

In response, she threw her head back against his shoulder. "That feels good."

"Oh yeah. But I think I've got the best of the deal."

He lathered on more soap, then slid his hands down her ribs. When he couldn't stop himself from doing what he really wanted, he brought his hands up and inward, lifting and lathering her breasts.

She sighed at his touch, then drew in a sharp breath when he glided his hands over her nipples.

The last time they'd made love, he hadn't been sure that he could trust her. Probably she'd felt the same way about him. But everything had changed. He knew what she'd been through. And he was going to make her future so much better.

Resting her head on his shoulder, she leaned back against him, then made a low sound when her bottom came into contact with his erection.

"Yeah, there's no way to hide that I'm turned

on," he said. "I can't help it with such a beautiful woman in my slippery hands."

From where he stood, he couldn't kiss her on the mouth. But he could nibble at her ear and play his lips along the side of her neck.

He'd thought that he could never love again. He'd been wrong. He longed to let Grace know that while he'd been acting as her bodyguard, he'd fallen in love with her. But he wasn't sure she could accept that yet.

She'd been made to feel less than human, but the good news was that she'd been part of a plan to fight back. And he was going to help her finish the fight. For her, and for all the others who had been caught in the trap created by Cortez and the Paladin.

As she molded her body to his, he slid one hand down the front of her, stopping to play with her navel before straying lower, into the tangle of dark hair at the juncture of her legs. Then he slipped even lower, into the plump, moist folds of her most intimate flesh.

She arched against him, and he kept up the

caresses, one hand playing with her breasts and the other taking long, gliding strokes through her feminine folds.

"Brady, I'm going to…"

"That's the idea, sweetheart."

He kept up his tender assault, pushing her up and up, until she tumbled over the edge, crying out as her body convulsed.

She leaned against him, warm and pliant in his arms.

"You're very sneaky," she whispered. "How long were you planning that?"

"I started thinking about it the moment we got here."

"And you sat through that meeting like you had nothing better to do than tell them about—"

He pressed his finger to her lips. "Let's not bring anyone else in here with us."

"You're right." She turned in his arms, grinning at him as she reached for the soap.

"Turnabout is fair play, don't you think," she purred as she clasped his erection with her soap-slick hand and began to stroke her fist up and down.

His indrawn breath brought another grin to her lips.

"You're going to…"

"That's the idea," she said, as she tightened her grip on him and moved her soapy hand up and down, bringing him to a rocking climax that had him calling out in pleasure.

Then he wiped the smug look off her face with a long, passionate kiss.

They stayed in the shower, washing each other, both of them absorbed in the delight of a very intimate water sport.

When they were both clean and fragrant, he turned off the water, grabbed a fluffy bath towel and dried her hair and body. After drying himself, he picked her up in his arms and carried her to the bed, where he began loving her all over again.

She rewarded him with small exclamations and with caresses that drove him to distraction.

When they had both reached the peak again, he settled down beside her, feeling more peaceful than he could remember. He had been emotionally dead for years, and she had brought him back to life.

It seemed as if he'd just closed his eyes when a knock at the door made them snap open again.

Beside him, he could feel Grace stiffen. "It's okay," he whispered. "We're safe."

She pulled the sheet up to her neck as she looked toward the door.

"Is something wrong?" he called out.

"We've located Kevin."

Brady sat up. "Okay. We'll meet you in the lounge in a few minutes."

They both climbed out of bed.

"He didn't call," Grace said, glancing at the phone she'd set on the dresser. "How did they find him?"

"I guess they'll tell us."

They dressed quickly, and Brady saw Grace

make a face in the mirror as she worked to get the tangles out of her hair.

"You look fine," he told her.

"I look like a mess. But I guess there are more important things to worry about," she added.

He watched her put on a businesslike expression to hide her emotions. He could imagine that had become a habit since she'd found out she was a clone. What had it done to Kevin Parsons? He hated to imagine it, knowing that John Ridgeway already had a boatload of problems.

They assembled in the lounge, where food had been set out.

As they ate, Brady looked around at the group. Some of the people he would have expected to see were missing, and he wondered if they had gone off on another assignment.

From the way the group was dressed, he gathered that they were going after Kevin.

And Grace was going with them, too.

"You know Kevin," Max explained. "If we run into trouble, we may need you."

She gave him a hard look. "I'm going, in any case. He doesn't know any of you. I can reassure him that you're on his side."

Brady nodded tightly. He didn't like bringing her along, but he knew she was right. "How did you find him?" he asked.

"We drew a circle on a map around Washington, DC, and started combing through real-estate records. We found a farm near Winchester that had been rented by Karen Hilliard."

"Good going," Brady answered. "But that doesn't prove Kevin is there."

"We've investigated the farm. There's someone living in the house. Either it's Kevin, or it's a setup. Because Kevin won't answer the phone, we need Grace to come with us and smooth things out."

Brady nodded, but he felt compelled to mention one more problem. "If you could find Kevin, so could the Paladin's men."

"Yeah," Max admitted. "Which is why we'd better get there before they do. We're going by helicopter again, but we'll land far enough away so that he won't hear the chopper. We have cars standing by."

"Who's down there?" Brady asked.

"Alex Shane. He left from the Eastern Shore of Maryland a while ago."

"And what exactly is the plan?"

"It's going to depend on the circumstances," Max answered.

Brady had lost his appetite, but he drank a cup of black coffee and grabbed a cinnamon bun on the way out the door.

As they hurried to the landing pad, he glanced at Grace and saw that her features were set. As her bodyguard and the man who loved her, he wanted to order her to stay at the Randolph facility. But he knew that success depended heavily on her.

They took off toward the south, and as they flew, they discussed several scenarios.

When he reached for Grace's hand, she

squeezed back, but he could see the tension on her face.

Alex was waiting for them on the road outside the farm.

"Any activity?" Brady asked when and they were all assembled near the entrance.

"No."

"Maybe he's cleared out," Max suggested.

"Not unless he belly-crawled across the fields in back of the house."

Brady couldn't hold back the thought circling in his head. "What if the Paladin's men got to him already and they're waiting here for us?

"The only way we're going to find out is for me to go in," Grace answered.

"You mean *us*. You and me," Brady said. There was no way he was letting her go in there alone.

"But he won't trust you."

He denied her objection. "He will if he thinks I'm putting myself at risk."

After donning bulletproof vests, Brady and Grace started up the farm road.

Giving her a fierce look, he said, "Stay behind me."

There were open fields on either side of the narrow drive, but they had been taken over by tall weeds and grasses. Brady could hear his own footsteps crunching on the loose gravel of the road surface.

Raising the bullhorn he was carrying, he said, "Kevin, this is Brady Lockwood, John Ridgeway's brother. We've come to get you to safety. Grace is with me. If you can hear me, come to the door. We mean you no harm."

There was no answer.

As they moved up the driveway, Brady imagined John Ridgeway in there, trying to figure how his brother would react.

"Kevin, this is Brady Lockwood," he said again. "I know you haven't answered Grace's phone calls. That's why we're here, to talk to you in person."

They were about fifty yards from the house, and he still saw no signs of activity. But as

Brady took another step, a shot rang out, and a bullet whizzed past his head.

Dodging to the side, he threw Grace into the weeds, then came down on top of her, protecting her with his body. There were no other shots. Perhaps it had only been meant as a warning.

"Is it him?" she whispered. "Or did the Paladin's men get here first?"

"I don't know."

"Green light. All right to get up," someone called out from the house, and Brady froze as he recognized the voice.

# *Chapter Fifteen*

"What the hell is going on?" Brady shouted.

"It's all right," the voice answered again.

Brady scrambled up and did a double take. A man who could be a younger version of his brother was standing in the doorway, looking daggers at him. Behind him was one of the Light Street men—Hunter Kelley.

"We got him," he said.

Brady gave him a hard look. "You mean, you got here hours ago, and you were using me and Grace as decoys while you got into the house and captured him?"

"Yeah."

"We could have been killed. He shot at us!"

"Miscalculation," Hunter said in a mild voice. "Sorry."

"You could have told us the plan."

"You would have behaved differently," Hunter answered, and Brady knew he was telling the truth.

Grace had also gotten to her feet and was standing beside Brady. Addressing Kevin, she said, "It's okay. We're here to help you."

Kevin turned toward her. "The hell you are! They broke into the house. Why should I trust them?"

"Because the man with you is a clone," Grace told him. "Like you and me. He's been a member of the Light Street Detective Agency for years. They trust him. He trusts them. And I do, too."

Kevin swiveled his head and looked at the man beside him. "You're a clone?" he said. "Prove it."

Hunter laughed. "I can't prove it. The man I'm cloned from died before I was…

manufactured at a secret government facility called Maple Creek. You were supposed to be used for spare parts. I was going to the Middle East on a suicide mission. Both of us are lucky that we ended up with Light Street instead."

Behind Brady, Max Dakota spoke. "We should get out of here while the getting's good."

"Do I have to keep a gun on you?" Hunter asked Kevin.

The younger version of Brady's brother shook his head. "I'll go quietly."

It was eerie how much he sounded like John Ridgeway. How much he looked like the man.

Hunter lowered his weapon.

"Let me get a few things from the house," Kevin said.

Brady hung back, figuring that this wasn't the time for any brotherly bonding, but Grace walked toward the porch. "Can I help you?" she asked Kevin.

"No. I'll be right there." He and Hunter disappeared, and Brady waited tensely for several minutes, until they came out again, both carrying duffel bags.

The contingent that had come with Brady and Grace returned to the car. Hunter and Max escorted Kevin to another vehicle. But they were all heading back to the Randolph compound.

Now that they were on their way back, he felt as if they'd taken care of the easy part. He knew what John Ridgeway was like. And getting Kevin to join them in the plan he'd devised was going to be the tricky part.

LATELY, CHARLES HANCOCK had spent too much time waiting beside the phone. This time, when it rang, he snatched up the receiver.

"Did you get him?"

"He was at the farm in Winchester."

He didn't like the way the conversation was starting out with a comment in the past tense. "And?"

"And he's gone."

Charles didn't permit himself a curse, not where an employee could hear.

"Did he leave by car? What?"

"A helicopter landed near the farm while we were on the way there. He could have left in that."

"He arranged it?"

"Don't know."

"Come back here, and we'll regroup."

"Yes, sir."

Charles hung up, wishing he could simply eliminate the men who had failed to bring him Lockwood and Cunningham. And now Kevin Parsons. But he didn't have that luxury, not yet.

Who would have the resources to whisk Parsons away in a helicopter?

He didn't know but he was going to find out.

AFTER THE HELICOPTER landed at the Randolph facility, Brady glanced toward Grace. He wanted to spend some quality time with her, but she immediately started talking to Kevin. And when she, Kevin and Hunter walked down the hall to the solarium, he knew that butting in was a bad idea. They all had something in common that he could never share. He was jealous, but he knew that if anyone could get through to Kevin, it was the other clones.

Hoping his features didn't reflect his mood, Brady went back to the lounge with the other agents.

"Have you made any progress locating the Paladin?" he asked Max.

"We have several candidates in mind," his friend answered.

"What are your criteria?"

"They have to be 'connected.' They have to have an unexpected source of money. They have to live in a secure location."

"That includes a lot of people."

"Yeah, but there are other factors. We're assuming he didn't hatch this plan strictly to make money. He's also into affecting public policy. And there's one more big clue—the e-mails of the people Grace told us about.

We should be able to see who they contacted before they had their operations."

"You can hack into their private e-mails?" Brady asked.

"Yeah. We'll nail him. Then we have to decide what to do."

"Why don't you tell us what you're planning?" The question came from Kevin.

Brady gave the young man a direct look. "A lot of it depends on you."

"Oh yeah?"

"See what you think about this idea."

JOHN RIDGEWAY'S funeral had been an ordeal, Ian Wickers thought as he strode into his den. And things weren't getting any better. After a long meeting with Patrick and Barbara Frazier, he needed a stiff drink. He poured himself two inches of Scotch, then downed half the liquor in one gulp. Feeling a little more in control of himself, he sat down in his easy chair and reviewed the day's events.

Lydia Ridgeway had been the model widow,

although Ian had known she was seething inside. She'd wanted a show of family unity, and Brady Lockwood had not cooperated.

In fact, Brady had vanished off the face of the earth. But that wasn't Ian's problem. Thank God, because he was busy dealing with Patrick and Barbara. He could manage Patrick all right. The man was unsure of himself and wanted guidance.

But Barbara was another matter. Lydia had sat back and let her husband deal with business affairs. Barbara was already showing up at Ridgeway Consortium meetings and putting in her two cents. And some of her comments made it seem as if she'd been planning this agenda for a long time.

He'd like to strangle the woman. Instead he kept a polite smile pasted on his face as he listened to her ideas and told her why they wouldn't work.

He downed the rest of the Scotch, then looked up as the door to his office opened.

"Mind if I join you?" a man asked.

He almost dropped the glass when he saw who was standing in the doorway.

"John?" he asked.

"You could say that."

"You...you're dead. We buried you three days ago."

"Yeah. Inconvenient, isn't it? It wasn't supposed to happen this way."

As the man moved farther into the room, Ian studied him. This was no actor pretending to be John Ridgeway. This was Ridgeway. He walked like Ridgeway, talked like Ridgeway, had that assessing Ridgeway gleam in his eyes.

Ian felt outrage bubbling up inside himself. He'd just gone through hell, and now it turned out to be a trick.

Standing up, he faced the invader with fire in his own eyes. "You faked your death?" he asked. "But why?"

John tipped his head to the side the way he so often did and gave Ian that half smile he'd perfected. It was obvious he was enjoying this surprise meeting.

"No. It's more complicated than that. Do you remember I was going to spend a few weeks at my vacation home in Jackson Hole?"

"Yes, right."

"I was going to have a secret operation."

"I didn't know that."

"Like I said, it was a secret. A heart transplant."

"What? You were going to do that—and not in a hospital?"

"I had to because it was going to be illegal." He paused a beat to let that sink in, then continued. "Illegal because the organ donor was my clone, raised to provide me with spare parts, if I needed them."

"Okay. I thought you really were John. But you've gone too far, whoever you are. That's preposterous. I don't believe it. What kind of trick are you trying to pull?"

"No trick. Only, things aren't exactly what

they seem. I'm not John Ridgeway. I'm his clone. He didn't get a chance to kill me."

Ian wavered on his feet as though he'd been socked in the chest. "What?"

"As you pointed out, John is dead. You saw his body, for Lord's sake. You read the autopsy report. You suspected he was murdered. They did it to save my life." As he spoke, he pulled out a cloth and began wiping makeup off his face.

Ian watched transfixed as John Ridgeway grew younger.

"A hard act to follow," another man said from the doorway.

Ian's gaze shot to the newcomer.

"But I think I've almost managed it," Brady Lockwood said. "I think you've been looking for me," he added as he stepped through the doorway. He was followed by an attractive woman whose appearance also made him goggle.

"Barbara?" he asked, the name coming

out as a gasp. "What the hell have you been up to?"

"I don't know. What *has* she been up to?"

"You're…"

"Her clone. Like my friend is Ridgeway's clone. I go by the name of Grace Cunningham. You've been looking for me, too."

Totally confused, Ian dropped back into his chair as he continued to stare at his visitors.

"I assume Barbara has been giving you a hard time," the woman named Grace Cunningham said. "Acting like she's going to personally take over the Ridgeway Consortium."

"Oh yeah."

Brady Lockwood stared at Ian with satisfaction. "You suspected there was a conspiracy to kill my brother," he said. "You were right. Only it's nothing like what you were thinking." In a level voice he began to lay out the facts for the Ridgeway chief of staff.

Ian listened transfixed, then flicked his gaze to the woman. Like "John," she had taken off her makeup. Without it, she also looked younger—and a lot less like Barbara Frazier.

"So now you know about the clone conspiracy," Brady said. "After Karen Hilliard told them who they were, they banded together to save their lives."

"It's hard to believe."

"I've brought you living proof. If you want, we can do DNA testing on...Kevin Parsons. That's the name his adoptive parents gave him. And on Grace. You'll see they're exact replicas of the originals."

Ian sighed, still trying to wrap his head around the new and disturbing information. "I guess you're not working an elaborate con on me. What do you want?"

"Your help. The doctor who created the clones is dead but the man who came up with this diabolical organ bank is still alive. He calls himself the Paladin. He doesn't know which of the clones are involved in the mutual protection society, so he's going after all of them."

"Who is he?"

"We've been trying to find out, and so far we've drawn a blank. We thought we could get his name from e-mails to his clients, but it's not working out. I'm hoping his name will be in my brother's records. The trouble is, I'm on Lydia's enemies list. I can't get near any of John's computers."

"How do I fit in?"

"I want you to get us in to see her."

"She'll never agree," Ian snapped.

"Obviously, you can't tell her you're bringing us. Maybe you can call and say you need to discuss her pension from the Ridgeway Consortium." He laughed. "Yeah, any threat to her income will get her attention."

"Then what?" Ian asked.

"Tell her that you'll be arriving incognito so as not to alert the press and that the gate-house should be prepared to let in a van from Woodley Flowers."

"A van from a flower shop? You're kidding?"

"No. That's how we arrived here, as a matter of fact. Don't let on that the three of us will be with you. And be careful what you say. Her phone might be tapped."

"Why?"

"Because the Paladin is looking for us. He might assume I'd try to get to Lydia. Which is another reason to go in with you."

"I'll do my best," Ian said as he picked up the phone and dialed. A while ago he'd been wondering if he'd have to quit the consortium rather than work for Patrick and Barbara Frazier. Now his prospects were looking up.

"LYDIA," HE SAID, when the widow came on the line. "I'm sorry to disturb you, but some important matters have come to my attention. I'm wondering if we could meet this evening. If you can see me, I'd appreciate it."

"It's something we need to discuss right away?" Lydia asked.

"Yes. It's a confidential matter—concerning your finances."

"Are they at risk?"

"I'd rather not say over the phone. If anyone's

with you, perhaps you should tell them you want to be alone."

"Yes. All right."

Feeling like an agent in a spy novel, he added, "To make sure the press doesn't get onto this, I'm arriving undercover. Tell your gatehouse I'll be in a flower delivery truck."

"This is a joke, right?" Lydia said.

"No. And thank you so much for seeing me, my dear," he added, signing off as quickly as he could.

After replacing the receiver, he looked up to see that Brady had moved to Grace Cunningham's side and put his arm around her. Interesting. Brady Lockwood had been in pretty bad shape after his wife and daughter had died. Now it looked as if he and Grace were an item. Well, good for him. He deserved some happiness.

But first he was going to have to survive Lydia's wrath. She'd mentioned Brady off and on over the past few days, and it had never been with affection. She was angry that he'd disappeared, and his failure to attend his brother's funeral was the last straw as far as she was concerned.

"LET'S GET IT OVER with," Brady muttered, pretty sure that the confrontation wasn't going to be pleasant.

They all got into the flower truck which had no windows but comfortable seats in the back. Max Dakota drove.

As they rode to the Ridgeway house, Brady tried to pretend that his stomach wasn't tied in knots. Last time he'd been there, he'd almost gotten shot.

But security was a lot different than it had been on his previous visit.

"Flowers for Mrs. Ridgeway," Max Dakota said, and the man in the guardhouse waved them through.

"Pull around to the back," Brady said, knowing the backyard was screened by trees and shrubbery.

Max parked in front of the four-car garage.

The maid let them in, eyeing Brady with alarm. Apparently the mistress had given her an earful about him.

"She's in the den. But she's not expecting you."

"She's not going to shoot me, is she?" Brady quipped.

"I wouldn't be too sure," the woman answered.

Lydia was sitting on the couch with a glass of Scotch in her hand. More Scotch, Brady thought as the smell wafted toward him. But it didn't affect him.

Lydia was wearing a floor-length royal-blue dressing gown, and her usually immaculate hair was mussed as though she'd run her fingers through it. Her husband's death had hit her hard, for a lot of reasons.

She looked up with a sad smile, prepared for a meeting with Wickers. When she spotted Brady, she stood and glared at him.

"You bastard. You left me alone when I

needed you. And now you dare to come here. What do you want?"

"You asked me to find out if your husband was murdered," he said in an even voice. "That put me in considerable jeopardy. I've been running for my life."

"Or drowning your sorrows in a bottle."

He wanted to say, "Like you." But he let that go and said, "I came to give you a report and to ask for your help in seeing that justice is done."

"Get out of here."

"We need to talk."

"So you tricked Ian into bringing you here?"

Up until then, Lydia's total focus had been on Brady. Finally, she looked at Grace—then Kevin.

When she saw him she gasped. "How dare you? Get him out of here! John asked you to find his illegitimate son, and you have the nerve to bring him to my house."

Fury contorted her face, and she ran at Kevin,

her fists raised. Brady caught her before she could hit the younger man.

"None of this is his fault. Leave him alone."

Kevin tipped his head to the side. "Now Lydia," he said. "You're getting yourself upset for the wrong reasons. Just settle down, and we can have a reasonable discussion."

She goggled at him, and Brady understood. He'd spoken to her as if he was John Ridgeway, in the same tone of voice.

"I'm not John's son," he said more gently.

"But…"

"You knew John was going to have a secret heart transplant," he went on. "At your Jackson Hole Ranch."

She answered with a small nod.

"Where did you think he was going to get a heart?"

When she didn't respond, he said, "You thought he was going to buy one on the black market."

She answered with a tight nod.

"Actually, before he was thirty, he bought a

special insurance policy. A clone he could use for spare parts. Did you know about that?"

"That's crazy."

"I'm that clone. I look like him. I talk like him. I have his DNA."

She shook her head in disbelief, and Brady was sure she hadn't been in on the plot. She wasn't a good enough actress to fake her reaction.

"His name is Kevin Parsons," Brady supplied. "He didn't know he was a clone until one of the others warned him. They were determined not to let John sacrifice Kevin, so they worked out a plan to save him."

"You mean kill John to save…his clone," she said in a gritty voice.

"They were protecting themselves."

Grace spoke for the first time. "And they had help from someone who wanted John out of the way,"

Lydia's head snapped toward her. "Who are you? You look familiar, but I can't place you."

"Because I had plastic surgery to disguise my appearance. I'm the clone of Barbara Frazier."

Lydia studied her. "Yes, I can see that—even with the alterations. Your eyes…"

"Barbara wanted John out of the way—to make room for her husband. So she helped us get access to John."

"You're the woman he was sleeping with! I sent Brady to find you. You're Grace Cunningham."

"I'm Grace. But I didn't have an affair with your husband. That was Karen Hilliard. You can think of her as Kevin's twin sister."

"No," Lydia said, but her voice was weaker now.

"I'll fill you in on all the details later," Brady said. "But I want your help now. We have to find the man who was responsible for…" He stopped and glanced apologetically at Grace "…for having the clones created."

"Why?"

"Because he knows about the conspiracy, but he doesn't know which clones are involved. So he's killing all the ones he can find." Brady gave Lydia a hard look. "The only name we have for him is 'the Paladin,' and we need your help to find him."

He could see her internal debate.

"John's scheme to kill Kevin was immoral. You can do the right thing by helping us find the man who hatched the whole plot."

"How?"

"The man acted as a gatekeeper for access to the clones. John told him he wanted a new heart. The Paladin decided he wasn't sick enough to sacrifice his clone. That's why John asked me to locate Kevin. John and the Paladin obviously had some correspondence, and I'd like to go through his computer and find it."

He held his breath, waiting for her answer.

Lydia lifted her chin. "I want something in return."

# Chapter Sixteen

"What are you demanding?" Brady asked.

"I knew Barbara Frazier was ambitious for her husband. I didn't know that would extend to murdering John. I want her punished."

"You don't mean in a court of law, do you?" Ian Wickers asked. "Because that would mean exposing what John did to ensure himself a perfectly compatible organ donor."

Lydia thought about that.

"I think we can arrange a suitable punishment," Wickers said.

"What?" Lydia demanded.

"Probably it's better if you don't know what

it will be. That way, you don't have to deny anything."

She considered that and nodded. "All right."

"I'd like access to John's computer," Brady said.

"It's in his office. I haven't touched any of his things." She looked at the others and offered a grudging invitation. "Make yourselves comfortable."

Grace looked at Brady.

"Go on," she said. "I'll stay here."

He wanted to keep her in sight, but he figured he'd better do the job he'd come for and get out. So he followed Lydia upstairs to his brother's office, sat down at the desk and booted the computer.

Lydia settled into an easy chair in the corner, watching him, and he wondered if she believed he was going to find evidence of her husband's murderous activities. Doing his best to ignore her, he went into John's e-mail, going back to the period just before his brother had asked him to locate Kevin Parsons.

A month before his meeting with John, he found an e-mail with the subject "Lifeline." The reply said, "Sorry. Access denied."

He was pretty sure the cryptic message was from the Paladin, but when he tried to find the name of the sender, he found it had gone to a mail clearinghouse that charged large fees to forward correspondence.

Brady had been in the computer field before he'd taken on the role of private detective, and he knew he wasn't going to get past the gatekeeper at that site. Hoping the rigid set of his shoulders didn't give away his emotions, he started scrolling farther back through his brother's mail, looking for the exchange between the two men.

He hit it lucky with some correspondence about a month before the denial, when John had contacted a company called Executive Traders, asking about ordering a replacement for his hard drive. Brady didn't recognize the company, which was interesting because his brother usually consulted him about computer-related problems.

He took down the name of the firm, then checked it out on the Web. It didn't sell computer hardware at all, as far as he could see. In fact, their business was financial services. Digging further, he saw that the initial request had been routed to the executive offices, where John had been given an "out of office" automatic reply. He assumed there had been some other contact after that, using a different method—culminating in the "access denied" reply.

There was a phone number, but he didn't want to call it because he didn't want an inquiry traced back to him—or to the Ridgeway household.

His next stop was the "about us" section of the Web site, where he scanned the names of the officers, but he couldn't tell much from the quick look.

"Where's John's laptop?" he asked Lydia.

She went into the bedroom and brought it back. "What do you want it for?"

"Additional research."

He booted it up, got the company's Web site and took the computer downstairs, where Wickers, Grace and Kevin were waiting.

"I think I might have a lead on the Paladin," he said.

When they all looked hopeful, he added, "But we need to make sure we've got the right guy."

After explaining the route he'd taken, he said, "We'll each take an officer of the company. Grace, you can use the Light Street laptop I brought along. Kevin, take this one. And I'll use John's computer upstairs. By going into the backgrounds of the officers of the company, we should be able to figure out which one is the Paladin."

After getting them started, Brady went back upstairs. Twenty minutes later, Kevin and Grace joined him.

"I think it's Charles Hancock," she said. "The vice president of the company."

"Why?"

She grinned. "Well, here are his political contributions," she said, showing him a very fringe Web site. "They match the kind of philosophy he's exhibited with the cloning project."

Kevin explained, "He has several different houses. But his base of operations is his McLean estate. Once Grace put me on to him, I used Google Earth to get a picture of the estate." He showed it to Brady. "His compound is heavily fortified. There's no reason the owner of a financial firm would need that kind of security. His real-estate taxes indicate that the property cost fifteen million dollars."

Brady whistled through his teeth. "A nice piece of change."

"And he's been spending a lot more money than the business brings in. Which says he has other sources of income."

"We both checked into his finances," Grace continued. "He owns several companies—

including one in the biotech field. One of the subsidiaries was Bio Gens."

"Where Cortez did his nasty little experiments," Brady said.

"Exactly."

"That pretty much nails it. Good going."

"But we can't go after him until we're positive," Grace said.

"Now that we have this information, we can put the Light Street Detective Agency on the case. I want to make sure he's the Paladin, and I want to know everything we can about him. I want to know how he thinks. How he'll react."

"We have a pretty good head start on that," Grace murmured. "He'll react with aggression."

"I believe we can use that."

"THERE'S BEEN SOME unusual activity at the Ridgeway Estate," Charles Hancock's chief of security informed him.

"Like what?"

"Delivery vans going in and out. Flowers. Catering."

"That's not so unusual, given that Lydia's husband just died and she's been having a lot of company."

"I've taken that into consideration. It's more than you would expect. And there have been several different companies."

"Let me see."

The man handed Charles a list, and he looked over the entries.

"You might have something here," he conceded. "What do you think is going on?"

"I think Brady Lockwood and Grace Cunningham have been sneaking onto the estate."

"For what purpose?"

"I don't know. But we may be able to nail them there."

"Or make Lydia Ridgeway tell us where they are."

"Her security is a lot more lax than it used to be."

"Okay. I want you to have a chat with Lydia. Tonight. I want to know everything she knows."

"I don't think that's going to be a problem."

THE RANDOLPH SECURITY facility was too far from the center of the action, so they'd moved from the western Maryland location to a safe house in American University Park, provided by the Light Street Detective Agency. It was on a quiet street, where they could easily keep track of the traffic. The two-story house was set well back from the curb. The backyard was shielded by a high fence. And there were an alarm system and cameras, which they were monitoring on a twenty-four hour basis.

Still, Grace was nervous.

She, Brady, Max and Hunter had settled in for a long wait, while they worked on plans for their next move. Common sense urged her to get out of town—far, far away from the Paladin. Yet she knew that wasn't really an option, not with innocent people dying.

"Here's another one," she said, pointing to an inside page of *The Washington Post*.

Brady took the paper from her and read an item about a young man who had been killed while riding his bike in Sligo Creek Parkway. The driver had hit him and sped off.

"You can't be sure that's the Paladin's work," Brady said.

"No. But there's a spate of fatal traffic accidents involving people in the right age range. And there's another item, about a murder during a burglary." She pointed to the front page of the Metro section.

"Can we prove any of it?" Brady asked.

"Yes," Max answered.

They both looked at him. "There was a wound on the arm of that robbery victim. I assume the killers stopped to remove the transmitter. And the same with the hit-and-run."

She dragged in a breath and let it out. "As far as we know, they're operating on the East Coast?"

Max shook his head. "There are some

suspicious reports from the Chicago area. We're assuming they also have an assassination team there."

"Have the police made any connection between the cases?" Brady asked.

"I don't think so. At least that's what my sources in the various departments are telling me. There isn't a pattern that they're going to pick up quickly if they're not looking."

Frustrated, Grace got up and walked to the window, where she stared out into the nicely landscaped backyard.

"I don't like living in comfort while the Paladin's killing people," she whispered.

Brady got up and stood behind her, wrapping his arms around her and pulling her back against him.

"I know," he whispered. "But we don't want to make a fatal mistake."

She nodded, knowing he was right, yet she was hardly able to deal with the wait.

"We should have some dinner," he said.

"I don't have much appetite."

"Neither do I, but you can't make yourself sick." He forced a laugh. "Of course, that might happen anyway if I fix the dinner."

"That's your ploy to get me to cook?"

"Yeah."

She followed him into the kitchen, praying that the wait would be over soon.

IT WAS JUST AFTER midnight when Lydia Ridgeway woke to find a large hand clamped over her mouth.

She'd taken a sleeping pill, and at first she thought the hand was part of one of the nightmares that had been plaguing her since John's death. The hand pressed harder, and she knew it was real.

A jolt of fear zinged through her. A man was in her bedroom. Although she couldn't see his face, she felt his malevolent presence.

The Light Street team had warned her that something like this could happen, and she'd dismissed the danger.

Now her heart started to pound as she struggled to sit up.

"Scream and I'll kill you," a harsh voice said close to her ear. "Do you understand?"

She nodded, and the hand was removed. A breeze blew on her face, and she knew it was from the window, which had been closed when she'd gone to bed. The beam of a small flashlight switched on, hitting her in the eyes, making her blink.

"How did you get in here?" she whispered.

The intruder answered with a harsh laugh. "Your security is a joke."

"What do you want?"

"Information."

"Like what?"

"Where are Brady Lockwood and Grace Cunningham."

"I don't know."

"They've been here."

"No."

"That's a lie." The sharp words were punctuated by a slap across her face.

Unprepared for the pain and violence, she whimpered.

"The Cunningham woman was having an affair with your husband."

Was that true? It wasn't what Brady had told her, yet they certainly had their reasons for lying.

"Were they here?"

"Yes," she answered.

"What did they want?"

"They wanted to find out about Karen Hilliard," she lied, hoping he would believe her.

"Where are they now?"

"I don't know."

"Not good enough." He gave her another slap, and she felt hot tears springing to her eyes.

"Leave me alone. I haven't done anything."

"You know where they are."

"No. He was too cautious for that. I mean, I don't know where they are, but I have a phone number. It's in the drawer." She fumbled at the bedside table and pulled out the pad of paper where she'd written the number. After handing it over, she trembled while she waited. This man could kill her now, and the maid would find her body in the morning.

He shined the light on the numbers. "This better be legit. Or you'll be sorry."

"It's the number. I swear."

"After I leave, don't call the cops. And don't call Lockwood to warn him."

"I won't."

"You'd better not. Or you're dead."

Sure that he had her totally cowed, he backed away, toward the window where he'd come in. When he'd left, she drew in a shaky breath, wondering what would happen next.

But that wasn't her concern, she told herself. She had survived, and she wanted to stay alive.

GRACE LAY RIGID in bed. Beside her, Brady slept, and she admired his ability to relax under the present circumstances. It was hard to believe that the Paladin's men weren't closing in on the house. The Light Street Detective Agency had left men here, but what if the Paladin's thugs came in a helicopter and dropped a bomb on the house?

*Stop it,* she ordered herself. *Stop imagining the worst possible things that could happen.*

She took a deep breath, then felt Brady's hand close over hers.

"Did I wake you?" she murmured.

"No. But since we're both lying here in the middle of the night maybe we can take advantage of the situation."

He raised up on one elbow, leaning over her, his warm breath feathering her cheek before his lips touched down on her for a sweet persuasive kiss.

When she'd been young, she'd imagined marriage and children as part of her adult life. Then Karen Hilliard had contacted her and shattered that image of herself.

Although she'd hardly been able to admit it, she'd thought of herself as less than human. That was why she'd been willing to let

herself be sucked into Karen's scheme. Instinct
had sent her running from the Ridgeway
Consortium, but she never would have survived on her own. Brady had saved her. More
than saved her. He'd made her want to live
again. She'd allowed herself to start imagining a future with him. Really, she ached for it,
yet she was afraid that it would all be snatched
away from her.

But if she was going to be wiped off the face
of the earth tomorrow, she'd grab what she
could with the man she loved now. She hadn't
told him how she felt because she didn't want
to put any pressure on him. But she could savor
what they had now.

She pulled him closer, increasing the pressure of her lips against his, then stroked her
hand down his back to his ass, pressing him
more tightly against her.

"I see you're fully awake," he murmured
against her mouth.

"Thanks to you." She caught one of his hands

and cupped it over her breast, smiling at his indrawn breath.

"Tell me what you want," he whispered.

She wanted a normal life with him, but she wasn't going to say that; instead she ran her hand down his body, finding his erection. After pressing her hand over him, she slipped into his shorts, wrapping her fingers around him. Gratified by his response to her, she brought her mouth back to his for a passionate kiss.

When their lips finally broke apart, they were both trembling. He was leaning over her, his hand stroking down her body, when his cell phone rang, and they both froze.

He sat up and reached for the phone.

"Hello."

"Brady Lockwood?"

"Yes. Who is this?"

"I'm called the Paladin."

Brady sat up straighter and switched on the light, then looked at Grace. "Did you hear that?" he mouthed.

She nodded.

"Who are you?" Brady asked, pretending he didn't already know the answer.

"That's not important. Is Grace Cunningham with you?" the Paladin asked.

She saw Brady swallow. Before he could answer, she reached for the phone.

"Hello?"

"Ah, Grace. I'm so pleased to be in touch with you."

"How did you find me?"

"That's proprietary information."

"If you have this phone number, you can figure out where we are."

"Possibly."

"Give me a number where I can call you back."

The man on the other end of the line hesitated.

"I'm going to hang up," she warned.

"All right." He gave her a number, and she wrote it down, then clicked the off button.

"You did good," Brady told her, reaching out to wrap his arms around her trembling body.

"I was terrified."

When Brady got up and started pulling on his clothes, Grace did the same.

A knock at the door made her jump, until the visitor identified himself as Hunter.

"That was Hancock," Brady called out to him.

"Yeah. I figured."

"We'll be dressed in minutes."

Both of them continued to pull on clothes. When she was wearing jeans and a tee shirt, she opened the door.

Hunter was standing in the hall, holding a cell phone. "This one's secure. You can call him back without worrying about his tracing the call."

She wished she could be as sure.

## Chapter Seventeen

"If he finds you, he finds me," Hunter told her as a way to reassure Grace and calm her fears. "So I'm betting my life on it."

Grace nodded.

"Let's go down to the living room, where we can all sit and be comfortable."

"Okay," she answered, glad that she had a few more minutes before she had to speak to the man again.

They went downstairs where she and Brady took the sofa. Hunter pulled up a nearby chair. Max continued to man the surveillance center.

Trying to keep her hand from shaking, she glanced at Brady. He put his arm around her and squeezed her shoulder.

"He thinks he has the advantage. He thinks he tracked us down. He doesn't know it was a setup and that Lydia was *supposed* to give him our phone number."

"I hope she's all right."

"She is. We've got a man at her house," Hunter said. "There was a video camera in the bedroom. He would have rushed in there if she was in danger."

Grace nodded.

"So just feed Hancock the information we agreed on."

She wanted to ask, "What if I screw up?" But she didn't voice her doubts.

"We'll be right here," Brady said. "Just make sure he doesn't know that you know his name. At least not until we're ready to spring that on him."

"Right." She dialed, then waited while

the phone rang. After three rings, Hancock answered.

"Hello," she said, hoping her voice didn't sound too shaky. When she glanced at Brady, he nodded, indicating that the volume was loud enough for him to hear. Max did the same.

"I can't tell where this call is coming from," Hancock said in an annoyed voice.

"That's the idea."

His tone turned threatening. "You may think that you can avoid me, but I'll find you eventually."

She took a deep breath and said, "That's what I'm afraid of. After you called, I started thinking, maybe we can make a trade with you."

"What can you possibly have that I want?" he asked.

"I have the names of the clones."

"I don't need the names. I have the trackers."

"Except on the most dangerous ones. The central committee. Karen knew about the trackers. She warned her inner circle to have them removed."

"If that's true, why didn't she give you that information? Why didn't she take hers out?"

"We had to take that risk, so you wouldn't know about the others. You might have noticed that I got away."

"Not Karen."

"You didn't use the transmitter to find her. You knew the Ridgeway Consortium had her. And you took her away from them—so you could kill her at that house in Frederick. And also me and Brady."

There was long silence on the other end of the line. "All right," he finally said. "I'll trade you the names for your own safety. Spill."

"We have to meet in person."

"I'm not willing to do that," he snapped.

"Then you can sit around wondering when the remaining members of her group will find you."

"You don't know who I am."

She gave Brady a parody of a smile before continuing. "Like you said, it's a matter of time before they figure it out. You can think of them as a suicide squad. They'll do what it takes to get to you."

Again, he was silent for several heartbeats. Finally he said, "I'll meet you at the George Washington Masonic Monument in Virginia."

"So you can set a trap for me?"

"No."

"I'm not going anywhere you pick," she said, looking at Brady. He gave her a thumbs-up sign and mouthed, "you're doing great."

She switched her focus back to the call as he asked, "What would you suggest?"

Did his voice sound a bit less confident?

"Somewhere we can both feel secure. A location where you can't have your men swoop down on me, and I can't do it to you."

"Like where?"

"What about Chain Bridge? That's open territory. You can come from the Virginia side. And I'll come from the Maryland side. Or we can switch directions. I don't care who comes from where, but we'll meet in the middle."

"How do I know you aren't setting a trap for me?"

She forced a laugh. "Oh come on. How could I? You just called me a few minutes ago. I don't even know who you are."

"True," he said smugly. "But you'll have your bodyguard, Brady Lockwood, lurking about."

"So what? We haven't had time to prepare anything. You can send your men to start monitoring the bridge right now. I can do the same."

"And when do you propose that we meet— now that we've agreed on a location?"

"Tomorrow morning. At two a.m. That way, neither of us has an advantage. We each have less than twenty-four hours to prepare." Her pulse pounded while she waited for him to reply.

"All right," he agreed. "You come from Virginia. Is that inconvenient? Are you in Maryland?"

Although her chest was tight with tension, she laughed again. "Nice try."

"We'll set up roadblocks to close off the bridge. At that hour, there won't be much traffic. Flash your lights to let me know you've arrived. I'll do the same. Then get out and come alone. We walk across the bridge. I give you the names, and you give me a signed paper saying that you'll leave me alone."

"Why would you trust me?"

"Because I'll put the paper in my safe-deposit box—to be sent to the FBI if I'm killed. Not only the paper, but everything I know about your whole scheme. Even if you sign a false name, they'll be looking for you. And *you* won't be safe. So we'll have a hold on each other."

"All right," he snapped, then hung up.

She clicked the phone off and looked at Brady. "How did I do?"

"Fantastically. He thinks he's the one who initiated the contact, so he feels safe with your suggestion about the bridge."

"Now we have make sure you don't get killed," Hunter said drily.

Grace's head snapped toward him and she looked at him, her eyes filled with fear.

"Nice way to put it," Brady said.

"I'm just being realistic about the danger."

"But we have a hidden advantage because we actually started setting things up at the bridge a couple of days ago," Brady said.

Grace hoped he was right. She had no illusions about her role in this, but she was willing to do it, just like she'd been willing to be Karen's lookout. She'd had her reasons for helping Karen. Her motivation was different now. She had no real future unless they took care of Charles Hancock. And she was also thinking that this meeting with the Paladin would atone for her role in John Ridgeway's death.

"We'd better go into planning mode," Hunter said. "Once Hancock is out of the way, we can get into his computer, get the names of the other clones and deactivate their transmitters."

She nodded, knowing how much was riding on their scheme. Still, she wished she'd had a little more time with Brady this morning, wished she had that time now.

"The rest of the team is standing by," Hunter said. "Including some of Wickers's men."

"They know why we're going up against Charles Hancock?"

"They don't know his name, but they know that he's the cause of John Ridgeway's murder."

"Not the direct cause," Grace reminded him, feeling the need to be absolutely honest.

"It's the direct result of his diabolical clone scheme," Brady snapped.

"But—"

"Let's not argue about it," Hunter suggested. "We've got to focus on making sure we're prepared."

"Yeah," Brady agreed. He turned to Grace. "That means I have to leave now."

"I understand."

He took her in his arms and hugged her fiercely, and she clung to him just as tightly, not even embarrassed that someone was watching them.

"It's a little hard to give up my bodyguard role," Brady whispered.

"I know why you can't stay with me."

"I'll see you as soon as this is all over."

"Yes," she whispered, praying that both of them came through the coming confrontation.

The whole scheme was dangerous—as dangerous for him as it was for her.

He stepped away, then headed for the front hall, where his gear was already packed.

As she watched him go, she had to fight the urge to hug him one last time.

THE NEXT TWENTY-FOUR hours were a period of frantic preparation for Grace, even more than her previous training with Karen.

The Light Street team had already made some vital preparations for her meeting with the Paladin, but the intensity revved up when they knew they had Hancock on the hook.

Still, it seemed like only a moment since

she'd put down the phone before they were crossing the Potomac on the Fourteenth Street Bridge and approaching from the south, toward Chain Bridge, where she was either going to save her brothers and sisters...or die.

"Are you ready?" Hunter asked as he slowed the car.

"I hope so."

"You don't want to get out on that bridge and suddenly realize there's nowhere to go except over the side."

Hunter never pulled any punches. The blunt observation made her shiver as she pictured the rushing water and sharp rocks far below. Depending on the recent rainfall the rocks would either be hidden or exposed.

Hunter pulled up just inside the barrier where a fake road crew of Light Street and Randolph Security men had blocked access to the bridge. The few motorists who wanted to cross at this hour in the morning would be angry, but that was better than getting caught in the cross fire.

As she stared out at the darkened landscape, she thought again of Brady. He had his own dangerous part to play in this carefully scripted drama, and she hadn't seen him since his hasty departure from the safe house.

Hunter flashed his lights several times. Answering lights flashed from the Maryland shoreline.

The Paladin had already arrived. If it was really him.

Beside her, Ian Wickers shifted in his seat. She didn't like him, but he'd agreed to work with the Light Street men, and she'd known he was loyal to John Ridgeway. Maybe he was doing this for his former boss, but she suspected that he had his own reasons for joining the team. Probably thwarting Barbara Frazier was high up on his list.

Both Hunter and Wickers wished her luck as she climbed out of the car. She was going to need it, but she didn't voice her doubts to either of them. As she wiped her sweaty hands on the sides of her jeans, she was thinking about what she had to do.

Peering into the darkness ahead, she saw the bulk of the bridge looming over the river. She knew that they were on a rocky stretch of the Potomac called Little Falls, to distinguish it from the mighty Great Falls which was farther upstream.

This was near the site of the first bridge across the Potomac because the river was narrower here than closer to the city. The structure had been replaced when previous bridges had either collapsed or been washed away. But the present one was built on stone pilings dating back to the 1870s.

It was too dark to see the river below, but she felt the crosscurrents of wind grabbing at her hair and clothing. She reached to steady herself by grasping one of the bars of the five-foot-high railing, then quickly drew her hand back as her fingers plunged into spiderwebs.

Her heart was pounding now as she strained

her eyes into the darkness, trying to make out a lone figure coming from the other side.

Although she couldn't see Hancock, she could imagine him walking relentlessly forward. Was he nervous? Or had he put his confidence in some plan that the Light Street men hadn't anticipated?

"Don't think about that," she muttered as she kept walking.

She and the Paladin hadn't agreed on flashlights, but she'd brought one. Stopping for a moment, she switched on the light and played it on the pavement in front of her, then began walking forward again, willing herself to stand straight and tall.

In the darkness, another light blinked on, and she pictured the Paladin with a flashlight in his hand. She couldn't tell how far away he was, but she saw the light coming toward her at a steady pace. As if he was out for a stroll on a fine evening.

The wind tugged at her again, and she fought a feeling of disorientation. Still, she kept

walking, her heart pounding as the gap narrowed between the two lights.

Once they'd discovered Hancock's identity,
they'd found pictures of him. He was in his
sixties with a head of curly salt-and-pepper
hair, but he looked a decade younger than his
age. She wondered if that was because he'd
received organ transplants. She didn't know,
but she was certain that he'd had clones made.
Why not? It didn't cost him anything. Maybe
he had a whole army of them.

A sickening thought struck her. What if he
wasn't the one here? What if he'd sent a clone
instead?

But this was an entirely different situation
than capturing a copy of yourself and putting
him to death. This was a mission that required
skill and cunning. Like Kevin Parsons impersonating John Ridgeway. The person would
have to want to do it. And why would he cooperate with Hancock?

For money? Because he thought he was the
man's long-lost son?

She tried to shut off that line of speculation, knowing it was only going to distract her.

But her mind kept working away on the problem. One thing she knew about Hancock was that he'd been treated for arthritis. That was something a clone wasn't going to fix, unless he started having limbs amputated and replaced.

She shuddered, wishing her thoughts weren't taking such repulsive leaps. But she couldn't help it, not when she knew these might be the last few minutes of her life. She wasn't going to fool herself. This could be a suicide mission, no matter how well the Light Street team had prepared.

As Hancock closed the distance between them, she studied his gait. To her relief, she could tell that it hurt him to walk. Either he was really Hancock, or he was faking leg pain. But why would he bother to do that since he was sure she didn't know his true identity?

When ten feet separated them, she stopped and tried to penetrate the darkness. She couldn't make out much, except that he was a bulky man wearing a sport coat.

"Let me see you," she called out over the sound of the wind.

"Why?"

"Curiosity. You masterminded this whole scheme. I'd like to get a look at your face."

"That shouldn't do any harm," he said, his tone smug, as he raised the light so that it illuminated his features from below, giving him a horror-movie quality. But she'd thought that about him all along.

"Who are you?" she called out.

"A man with a mission." Lowering the flashlight, he asked, "Did you bring the names?"

"Yes. Did you bring a piece of paper swearing that you won't go after me?"

"Yes. Hand over the names."

"Hand over the safe conduct."

"I don't have any objections to going first," he said, his voice confident as he reached inside the pocket of his sport coat and brought out a piece of paper, which he held toward her.

She reached into the pocket of her jean jacket and pulled out her own paper. It was a list of ten names, but they weren't clones, so far as she knew. The Light Street men had made them up, plucked them at random from tombstones in several Baltimore graveyards, so that nobody would get hurt if this all went the wrong way.

But it wouldn't, she told herself fiercely as she and Hancock stepped toward each other, each holding what they'd brought. She was close enough to kiss him, she thought, if the contact wouldn't have made her sick.

He took the paper from her and unfolded it, shining the light on the list.

"Thank you," he said, more loudly than he needed to, and she was pretty sure that was a signal to the men who were waiting to get him out of this situation. "You think the FBI could find me if you died, but I'm planning to disappear. Nobody will be able to find me because I have the resources to create a whole new identity."

"But you haven't disappeared, and you're Charles Hancock," she answered.

To her satisfaction, he sucked in a sharp breath. "Where did you get my name?" he demanded in a voice that had lost some of its smugness.

"We've had it. We just weren't prepared to tell you—until now."

"I was careful."

"Yes. But we're not as stupid as you think we are."

"It won't do you any good," he answered sharply, and she knew he was scrambling desperately to wrest back control of the situation. He'd come here because he thought he had her completely boxed in. Now he was finding out that he'd made some dangerous assumptions.

Still, he intended to be the winner of this contest. "I'll be leaving here soon, and you won't," he added, pulling a gun from under his sport coat.

## Chapter Eighteen

In the distance Grace could hear the drone of helicopter blades, the sound making her scalp prickle. That couldn't be the Light Street men. It must be Hancock's team coming in for the kill. Fighting the impulse to turn and run, she kept her tone even as she said, "Before you shoot me, you might want to know a few things."

"What could you possibly tell me that's still of interest?"

"How about—your thug's getting our phone number from Lydia was a setup. We already knew who you were before you 'forced' her to talk."

"Oh come on. There's no way you could have figured out my identity."

"Sorry. You hid your trail, but not well enough. When Brady combed back through John Ridgeway's e-mail, he found some correspondence with a company called Executive Traders."

She saw a flash of reaction on the Paladin's face.

"From the messages, it looked like John wanted to buy computer software, but that's not what the company sells. That was a mistake on your part."

Hancock cursed under his breath.

"Brady began investigating the company officers, and you fit our specs for the Paladin. As soon as we knew who you were, we started setting up this location. Everything at this meeting is being videotaped. If you shoot me, the tape goes right to the police and the FBI—with the name Charles Hancock attached—along with an account of your clone scheme."

"You're bluffing," he spat out. "I've had my

men all over this bridge. There's no recording equipment here." But he didn't sound as sure of himself as he had been a few minutes earlier.

"The cameras aren't on the bridge." She gestured toward the houses on the cliffs above the river on the Virginia side. "We told the home-owners we were covert government agents running a sting operation. They were very happy to cooperate. The cameras are in their windows, and you're facing right toward them. Nice of you to approach from Maryland. But then we assumed you wouldn't let me have my first choice."

The gun in Hancock's hand wavered.

They'd been alone high above the river. Suddenly hooks clanked over the steel railings, and a group of figures began clambering up.

They were dressed in silver-gray jumpsuits with hoods, their outfits blending perfectly with the wide steel girders supporting the structure of the bridge so that they had been virtually invisible as they'd waited below the meeting place.

Brady, Max Dakota, Jed Prentiss and a fourth man whose face was covered surrounded the Paladin, just as the helicopters above them came swooping down.

Hancock waved frantically at the chopper hovering overhead. "Get me out of this," he shouted, although there was no way for the pilot to hear him.

Before the helicopter could get any closer, the Light Street men aimed machine guns upward and began firing. As bullets whizzed around him, the chopper pilot decided he hadn't signed up for a suicide mission and pulled abruptly away.

"No, come back!" Hancock screamed after the departing machine. When he saw they were leaving him, he darted forward, grabbed Grace and backed up, so that he was pressed against the railing.

"Come any closer and she dies."

As she felt the cold steel of a gun barrel against her neck, Grace's eyes met Brady's.

"Back up," Hancock shouted.

Brady and the Light Street men obeyed.

Could she dive for the surface of the bridge? Throw Hancock off balance? Or was her best bet waiting this out?

She knew from Brady's expression that he was trying to tell her something, but she didn't know what it was. Time stretched as the longest seconds of her life ticked by. Perhaps the last seconds. She saw the anguish on Brady's face, knew that he wanted to throw himself at Hancock. But that would only get her shot, so he stood frozen in place.

The fourth man who had come up from the underside of the structure started to pull off his hood as he took a step forward.

"Don't move. Stay back," Hancock shouted.

The man stopped walking but continued to remove the hood.

When the Paladin saw his face, he gasped, and Grace felt a shiver go through him. "No. You're dead," he whispered.

"You wish I were."

It was Kevin, wearing makeup, doing his

John Ridgeway impersonation again, and Hancock was too off balance to realize it might be the man's clone.

"Stay back. If anything happens to me, my men will still go after the clones," he shouted. "I mean the ones who have the trackers."

Kevin ignored him, speaking as though he were John Ridgeway. "Why should I care about that? When you denied my request for a transplant, what did you think would happen?" he demanded, his voice edged with anger. "I guess you didn't consider that I'd stage my death so I could get to you."

"No," Hancock wheezed.

With the man's focus on Kevin, Grace wrenched out of the Paladin's grasp and rolled away, praying that he wasn't going to shoot her.

It was clear she'd become a minor distraction. Hancock's full attention was on Kevin as he aimed his gun at the clone. "Stay back or I'll shoot."

"We want to take him alive," Brady warned.

"Never!" Hancock shouted.

As Grace watched in horror, the Paladin turned and vaulted over the railing. Both she and Kevin made a grab for him, but it was too late. His scream echoed through the river valley as he plunged toward the rocks below.

They all stood in stunned silence. The man would have hunted her down to the ends of the earth, but when he knew he had lost, he took control of his destiny.

The first to speak was Kevin. "Good riddance. I made him think I was angry about his denying Ridgeway's request, but it was his whole nasty scheme that turned my stomach."

Grace had started shaking, and Brady rushed to her side and pulled her close. "You were magnificent," he said.

"I was scared."

"So was I," he admitted. "For you."

"And I was scared for you. I was afraid Hancock's men would see you getting into position."

"We used an 'auto accident' to block off the

bridge for ten minutes. That was all the time we needed."

Still hardly able to believe she was free of the Paladin, Grace watched the Light Street team begin to remove their equipment from the bridge.

Wickers had joined the group. "Impressive work," he said.

Kevin nodded in agreement, then reminded them that the mission wasn't over. "We need his computer to get the names of the clones who have the transmitters."

Phil Yarborough, one of Wickers's operatives, had joined them. "His men have already killed some of them," he said dismissively.

Grace gave him a narrow-eyed look. She'd seen him around the Ridgeway Consortium, and she'd never liked him. Now he was confirming her opinion.

"Including Barbara Frazier," Wickers said.

"What?" she gasped. "She's no clone."

"But Hancock's men didn't know that."

Grace started to say more, but Brady gave

her a warning look and she clamped her lips shut.

"How did that happen?" Brady demanded.

Wickers gave him a satisfied look. "When you explained that she was the mastermind behind the plot to kill John Ridgeway to clear the way for her husband's taking over the Ridgeway Consortium, I started thinking about poetic justice."

Yarborough took up the narrative. "We got to one of the dead clones and removed the transmitter. Then we had the transmitter transferred to Barbara Frazier's purse."

"Hancock's men tracked it. They didn't know it wasn't actually on her person. But it proves that they're still out there operating."

Grace stared at him, stunned, as she took in the cold-blooded comment.

It was Brady who finally spoke. "We didn't hear anything about it on the news."

"I had it kept quiet," Wickers said. "Out of respect for her husband."

"Yeah."

"We'd better get that list," Grace said.

"Hancock's estate is fortified. What if we meet resistance?" Kevin asked.

Yarborough answered, "His men were here because this is where he needed them. And he expected to come back victorious."

"Still," Brady said, "there could be guards waiting for us." He looked at Grace. "I'm not letting you get anywhere near the place until we know it's safe."

"Not acceptable. As soon as news of his death hits, the estate will be sealed, and we'll never get the names."

"It's probably safe enough now," Wickers answered with a dismissive wave of his hand. "The men who came in the helicopter saw him kill himself. Without him, there's nothing for them to protect. They'd bail out—to save themselves."

The conversation was interrupted by Max, who came trotting back from the far side of the bridge. "I have something you need," he said holding out his hand. "The remote that opens his gate."

Yarborough reached for it. "I'll take that."

"You're coming with us?" Brady asked.

"Wouldn't miss it."

BRADY SLUNG HIS arm around Grace's waist and led her back the way she'd come a few minutes ago, thankful that she hadn't gotten hurt—or worse. They stayed close together. When he clasped her hand tightly, she squeezed back. He wanted to turn and kiss her, to tell the world that she belonged to him, but he knew the Light Street men and Kevin were right behind them, and he knew she'd be embarrassed by such a bold display.

They went in two cars, with the Ridgeway guys roaring into the lead.

"They're acting like this is their operation," Kevin muttered.

Brady was equally annoyed, but he'd worked with Wickers before and he knew the man had a tendency to take over. With effort, he kept his voice even. "We can use the help."

They followed the lead car toward the Hancock estate. Yarborough, who was driving, pulled up at the gate. Brady assumed he was using the remote, but it didn't seem to work, so he and Wickers got out and approached the controls that were on a nearby post.

When Brady started to get out, Grace put a hand on his arm. "They were so hot to take over, let them do it."

He gave her a questioning look.

"Stay with me," she whispered.

The urgency in her voice kept him beside her.

After a brief consultation, Yarborough strode back to the rear of his car and opened the trunk. Moments later, he was back with a crowbar with which he attacked the gate-locking mechanism.

As they tugged on the pry bar, a volley of shots rang out, and they fell to the ground.

"Down," Brady shouted, pushing Grace

toward the floor of the car and throwing himself on top of her. Long seconds passed with no more shooting.

Finally, they stirred.

"Everyone all right?" Brady called out.

Grace and Kevin both answered in the affirmative.

"Stay down."

When he looked out the window, he saw two bullet-riddled bodies sprawled in a pool of blood. Contrary to his orders, Grace was sitting up, following his gaze.

"Are they dead?" she whispered.

"Looks like it."

Brady eased the door open.

"Don't go out," she begged, fear piercing her voice.

"We can't stay here forever." He kept low and dashed to the side of the stone gatepost.

Still, his heart was pounding as he raised up to have a look at the control panel. After studying the keypad, he pressed a button and ducked back around the post.

But this time, the gate opened and there were no shots.

"What happened?" Kevin asked as he got out of the car.

"I think the fire was from an automatic system designed to kick in if the remote was used without pressing the all-clear button."

Grace joined them and asked, "How did you know which button to push?"

"I'm an electronics expert, remember?" He pulled out his phone and called Max Dakota. "We ran into a little problem at the Hancock estate. Can you send some reinforcements?" he asked, then explained what had happened.

Grace looked out at the dead men on the ground.

Brady followed her gaze, then reached for her hand and held on tight. "That could have been me. How did you know?"

"After you left to go down to the bridge, I kept reading up on Hancock. I…knew he was super security conscious. And he liked to be tricky."

"But you went to the meeting anyway."

"I had to."

He swallowed and tightened his grip on her hand, longing to take her off somewhere alone. But they still had work to do.

They waited beyond the gate until several of the Light Street men showed up, then all proceeded cautiously up the driveway.

"Stay here," Brady said again when they reached the house.

She shook her head. "I'm going to take the same risks as you."

Before he could stop her, she climbed out of the car, her gun in her hand, and he hurried to get in front of her, also with his weapon drawn.

At least he got inside the door first. Behind him, he heard Kevin say, "Let's not get in the way of the professionals."

It was so much like one of John's comments that Brady wanted to turn around and grin, but he kept his vision—and his mind—on the task.

He and the Light Street men hurried through the house, making sure it was clear and that there were no booby traps. It seemed Wickers had been right about the security force. They'd melted away when their boss had jumped off the bridge.

Brady came back to the front hall. "All clear."

"I want the names of the clones," Kevin said in a tight voice. Grace nodded in agreement.

Brady led them back to the Paladin's office, where a computer sat on the desk.

"Is it password protected?" Grace asked.

"Maybe." Brady sat down and touched the keyboard, then made a tsking sound. "But he thought he was coming right back, so he left it on for us."

"Sweet of him," Grace murmured.

He began searching the files. Because computer hacking was his specialty, it took only a few minutes for him to find what they were looking for.

"I've got it," he announced.

"Thank God," Kevin answered. "We've got to get to them as soon as possible."

"You really think Hancock's still got men looking for them?" Max Dakota asked.

"For their sakes, we have to assume he was telling the truth about that," Grace said.

"Why would they do it—if they didn't even come back here to defend him?" Kevin argued.

"He could have convinced them that the clones would come after *them*. Or he could have set up a bank account that pays out every time they provide proof of death," Brady answered.

"You've been thinking about it."

"Yeah."

"Well, you have the resources of the Light Street Detective Agency," Max said.

"Can we start looking for them now?" Grace asked anxiously.

Max gave her a sympathetic look, then addressed Brady. "Send the computer file to Light Street, and we'll get right on it."

"Thank you," Grace breathed.

It was getting light when they left the estate. As they drove back toward the bridge, Brady heard police sirens.

"I guess someone's discovered the body," Grace murmured.

"Or maybe just the car on the Maryland side, where parking is illegal. They'll want to know what it's doing there."

"What's next?" Kevin asked.

"Why don't you wait for us at the safe house where Grace did her prep work?" Brady suggested. "That's probably the best thing for now—until things shake out a bit."

As Kevin looked at him, time stretched taut. Finally the young man said, "Sure. I'll be waiting for your call."

Brady eased out a breath. He'd wondered if John's clone would listen to him. It seemed that he would.

They settled Kevin at the safe house. Grace waited in the living room while the two men spoke. He also made a quick, private phone call.

"I hope Kevin will be okay," he said as they climbed back into the car.

"He's taking your advice," Grace answered. "That should help." She cleared her throat. "You've got a chance to reverse your roles. Now you're the older brother."

He gave her a startled look. "Is it so obvious I was hoping for something like that?"

"No. But we were both thinking it. You have a lot to offer him."

"I hope so."

As they headed for Connecticut Avenue, he saw the tension in Grace's shoulders. Probably she thought they were returning to his apartment, but he didn't want any bad memories to interfere with the conversation he meant to have. Instead, he turned on Woodley Road.

When they pulled up at the Marriott Wardman Park, Grace gave him a questioning look.

"I haven't had a chance to get my apartment cleaned—since we tied up those thugs."

"That seems like a million years ago."

"We can stay here for a few days," he said, as he ushered her to the front desk, where he'd already made arrangements for accommodations in the elegant section of the hotel—the original Wardman Towers, that had been built early in the previous century.

When she stepped into a small suite with high ceilings and Chippendale furniture, she sighed. "This is beautiful."

"I was hoping you'd like it."

"Isn't it expensive?"

He laughed. "Apparently, I'm rich now. My brother left me a lot of money in his will. Probably to assuage his guilt at using me."

He didn't want to keep talking about John. He'd brought Grace here to be alone with her.

"Come here," he said, reaching out and folding her into his arms. He held her tightly for heartbeats, then eased away, far enough so that he could look down into her questioning eyes.

"I love you," he said.

Her breath caught. "You can love someone like me?"

"Like what?" he asked.

"A...clone."

"Did you think that would make a difference to me?" he asked softly.

"I...didn't know."

"You know I went to pieces after Carol and Lisa died. You know I was only half alive."

"And your brother rescued you. Then I helped kill him."

"You took a perfectly logical course of action to save Kevin's life. And you took a terrible chance with your own life."

"Still..."

Before she could protest further, he continued quickly. "John rescued me for his own reasons. Not because he cared about me. He knew I'd be grateful, and he knew he could use that. He had me doing a lot of dirty jobs for him. How do you think I felt when I realized I was the one who'd found Kevin for him?"

She winced. "You didn't know."

"But as soon as I found out, I got on the right side of the issue. The ethical side."

When she nodded, he kept his gaze steady on her. "The question is, how do you feel about me?"

Without hesitation she answered, "I love you."

"Thank God."

"But—"

He stopped her protest by lowering his mouth to hers for a long, passionate kiss. When he finally raised his head, they were swaying in each other's arms. Still, he saw the look of doubt in her eyes.

"What are you thinking about now?"

"My parents. They believe I'm dead. I want to get back in contact with them, but I don't want to give them a heart attack. And…and I don't know how much to say. Do I tell them I'm a clone? Do I tell them I was involved in a very nasty scheme?"

"It will help pave the way for your reunion

if a private detective visits them first and explains that he's located you."

"You mean you?"

"Yes."

She nodded eagerly. "That would be a good way to break it to them gently that I had to disappear for a while."

"To protect them because you were on a dangerous assignment for the government."

"That last part's a lie. This wasn't a government operation."

"No, but it would give you a plausible reason not to answer a lot of questions. Think about it. At the very least, it would ease their minds."

"I don't know if I can tell that kind of fib."

He laughed.

"What?"

"You let yourself get entangled in a web of lies. You made up a fake persona."

When she nodded tightly, he went on. "We don't have to work out every detail today. Right now I want to know one thing. Will you marry me?" He held his breath, waiting. He wanted to force the right answer out of her by kissing her senseless, but he didn't allow himself to do that. It had to be her decision.

When she answered, "yes," he let out the breath he'd been holding, then folded her close again.

"I want to make you happy," he murmured. "Give you the wonderful life you deserve."

"I have you. That's all I need." Her eyes were shining with happiness as she looked up at him. "We're two people who know what it's like to reach rock bottom."

"And come back," he added, daring to unleash his own happiness. "Let's go find the bedroom, because I want to start celebrating the first day of the rest of our lives."

\* \* \* \* \*

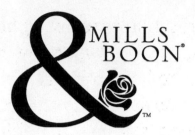